THE ETHER IN THE ENTRYWAY

COURTNEY MCFARLIN

1

*T*he wind whipped through the open windows of my car and I briefly wished I'd stopped by my house to grab a sweater before coming here. I rubbed my arms and rolled the windows up, noticing that Bernie, my cat, was currently staring at the historic building where we parked. I reached out to smooth the fur on his back as I looked out the window with him.

"What's up?"

"There's something very wrong here, Brynn."

In case you're wondering, yep, I can talk to Bernie and he can talk back. This was a relatively recent development for us, and we were still figuring out how everything worked. Honestly, not much had changed. He still ran the house with an iron paw, but at least now I could understand what he wanted. He looked at me with his emerald eyes and blinked slowly. My heart melted a little as I looked at his sweet little face.

"What do you think is wrong?"

"I can't tell from here, but it's a good thing Bob called you about this place. I'll go inside with you, of course."

"Of course," I said, trying to be nonchalant even though my stomach felt like the bottom dropped out of it.

Bob's a local realtor who had referred me to my last client. I'd wrapped that job up a few days ago, and was still trying to come to terms with the murderous family and two ghosts I'd run into.

That's right, I said ghosts. I not only talk to my cat, but I can also see and communicate with ghosts. It's a lot to take on good days, and let's just say the past few weeks haven't been filled with many of those. The Graff family had surprised me in more ways than one, but luckily, I'd come out of the experience unscathed.

Bob Tremaine was well aware of my strange abilities, and he thought I was the only one who could help his friend who owned the Maddison House, a local museum, where we were currently parked.

"Well, let's get this done. I'm getting hungry," Bernie said, stepping carefully into my lap.

"I wonder if any of the resident ghosts will be around?" I asked as I opened the door and watched as Bernie jumped onto the concrete and stretched.

The Maddison House had gained the reputation of being one of the most-talked about haunted places in our area. Deadwood, SD was home to many places who tried to claim the fame of having ghosts, but I knew for a fact that this place was legit.

Bernie was silent as he followed me around the car and wound his tail around my ankles. I stopped to look at the building, appreciating its architecture. My day job, if you will, is running an interior design and home staging company, even though my side hustle of assisting ghosts seemed to take up more time these days. I was a sucker for Victorian architecture, and luckily, this area was chock full of homes, just like this one.

The Maddison House's claim to fame, other than its ghosts, was its huge brick turret. I smiled as I walked up to the front door, eager to see the inside of the place. It had been years since I'd visited, and back then, I had paid little attention to the decor.

I pulled open the door as a gentle chime filled the air and felt Bernie's fur brush against my leg. I didn't know how he did, and he sure hadn't told me, but somehow, he disappeared from other people's view when he didn't want to be seen. One of these days, we were going to have a talk about it.

"Hello, welcome to the Maddison House," a woman said as she entered the small foyer.

I opened my mouth to answer, but stopped when I felt a deadly chill work its way down my back. Time seemed to slow as my muscles tried to move, but it felt like they were clamped in a steel vise. The woman looked concerned as her mouth moved in what I hoped was a fervent prayer. If my lips could have moved, I would have joined her. Slowly, the feeling passed, and it felt like real life was back at normal speed.

I blinked, never more glad that I had control of my lids again, and leveled a look at the woman standing across from me. Her wispy blond hair looked like it had been caught escaping the bun it was pinned into, and her faded blue eyes looked quizzical as she watched me.

"Are you okay, dear? I was talking to you, but you didn't answer me."

I let out a shaky laugh and tried to play it off. Was it possible she hadn't felt what had just happened?

"Sorry, my eyes didn't want to adjust, I guess. I'm Brynn Sullivan. I'm here to see Russ Givens."

She brightened and motioned for me to follow her. I glanced around, hoping to spot Bernie's coal black fur, but he wasn't in sight. I hoped whatever had frozen me hadn't gotten to him. She stopped in front of a beautifully carved door and rapped twice on it.

"Mr. Russ, Brynn Sullivan is here. I brought her back like you instructed."

"Please, come in," a jovial voice sounded from the other side.

I nodded at the woman and pushed open the door, revealing an ornate office that was chock full of antiques. My fingers were itching to examine the clock on the desk as I sat across from Russ.

His hair was a rusty shade of brown, shot with gray, and his eyes friendly as he held his hand out for me to shake.

"Thank you for coming," he said, pausing for a beat. "That will be all, Norma."

I heard footsteps moving down the wood floors of the hallway as Russ relaxed into his seat.

"Bob Tremaine asked me to stop by. He said you were having some, well, issues?"

I could have beaten around the bush, but I was almost completely sure Russ was at least passingly familiar with the paranormal. After all, he worked at a place renown for its ghosts. It was a relief, in a way. Usually, I had to do a complex dance around the subject and after what I experienced in the entryway, I didn't feel like performing.

"Right to the point, I like it," he said, letting out a half-laugh. "You are correct. We are having issues and honestly, I don't know how to explain it. Bob mentioned your abilities when I talked to him. He was adamant that you could help me."

I gave him a reassuring smile and nodded.

"I sure hope I can. Why don't you tell me what's been going on?"

Bernie brushed against my leg again, and I suppressed a jump. At least I sure hoped it was Bernie. I focused my attention on Russ as he leaned back in his chair and pursed his lips.

"Well, as I'm sure you know, although we are a museum of sorts, most people visit this place hoping to spot one of our resident ghosts. Bob said you're a local, right?"

"I am. I live in Gilded City, but I've done a lot of work in Deadwood."

He nodded.

"Bob assured me you would understand. Anyway, everything was fine until a few weeks ago. Our resident ghosts are, well, I'd have to describe them as gentle. They move a few things, and you can hear footsteps, but in all my years of managing this place, I never felt threatened."

He went quiet, and his kind brown eyes were troubled as he looked at me.

"And that changed?" I asked.

He nodded and cleared his throat.

"Yes. I don't know what happened, but it's getting worse. People who come here, they're looking for the experience of visiting a haunted mansion, but they're not expecting to get thrown around like they're in a horror movie."

My breath caught in my chest. This was not good.

"That's happened?"

"More than once. We're getting critical reviews on the internet, and people are staying away. The foundation that runs this place is small, and doesn't have much money. We rely almost entirely on the donations people leave and the small entrance fee we charge. If that goes away, I'm afraid we'll have to close our doors. There's been talking of selling the place and closing it down. Permanently."

His Adam's apple bobbed up and down, but he said nothing else.

"You said this started a few weeks ago. Was there anything that you feel started the problem?"

Russ leaned back in his chair and tapped on his chin, lost in thought. He finally shrugged and shook his head.

"Not that I'm aware of. Everything was fine, and then suddenly, well, it wasn't fine anymore. To tell you the truth, I think our resident ghosts are scared, too. No one has heard a thing in the past week, other than whatever else is going on. I know I probably sound crazy, but I just don't know what to do."

I held up my hand.

"You're not crazy. There are paranormal creatures all around us, and even if you can't see them or sense them, it doesn't mean they're not there. I will do everything I can to help. Will it be possible to visit after hours? I've found that a lot of ghosts prefer not to be too active when there are many people around."

Bernie leaned into my leg, and I could feel the vibrations of his purr through my pants. He didn't need to speak at that moment. I knew what he was feeling. I was proud of myself, too. I'd gone so long being ashamed of what I could do, and now it felt like I was finally coming into my own.

He nodded so hard his hair fell over his forehead.

"Absolutely. I'll give you the access code. I don't know what you normally charge, but we'll pay you. The foundation..." he said, trailing off and making a face.

"Don't worry about the payment," I said. "I can't make any promises, but I will do what I can. Do you mind if I walk around a little?"

"Do whatever you need to do. If you think it's necessary, we can close for a few days."

"You know, that might be necessary. If it is, you could say you're closing temporarily for some renovations. Given what I do, that wouldn't raise any suspicion," I said.

"That's right. Bob said you were an interior designer. If you feel it's necessary, we'll do it. We're not getting many people coming in, anyway. I can give Norma a few days off."

"I'll look around now and come back, probably tomorrow after you close, and we can figure it out from there," I said.

His smile was genuine as he reached across the desk again and shook my hand.

"Pleasure meeting you. I really appreciate this. If you need anything," he said, swallowing hard. "I'll be happy to assist."

"It should be okay. I'll be in touch."

I walked out of the office and looked down the hall. Not much had changed since my prior visit years ago, but I wanted to get a feel for the place. I headed back to the front and smiled at Norma.

"Russ said it was okay for me to look around," I said.

"Go ahead, dear. I'm just finishing up for the day. Are you going to be long?"

I noticed her glance at the clock and wished I'd been able to come earlier in the day. It was obvious she wanted to go home.

"No, just a few minutes. I won't keep you," I said, giving her a wave as I went up the stairs.

Even though it was a Victorian home, some updating had been done along the way. The main level had been opened up, and I briefly imagined what it would have looked like when there was a proper parlor. I kept going and looked at the bank of doors that stretched along the back wall of the building. I wasn't in any hurry to repeat my experience when I walked in, but I was definitely intrigued by what was going on.

I opened the first door I came to and stuck my head in. A four-poster bed dominated the small room, and I smiled when I saw they'd stuck with the original period fabric that had been popular in the early 1900s, shortly after the house was built. My inner design nerd cheered as I walked in and felt the wallpaper. They'd kept that authentic as well.

I walked around the bed and looked out the windows into the back courtyard. Even though the sun was starting its descent, the outdoor space felt cheery and welcoming. I felt the hair on the back of my neck rise as the temperature in the room dipped. Bingo.

I turned around and did a double take when I spotted my cat lounging on the bed. Leave it to Bernie to find the most comfortable spot in a room. I was just about to tell him to get off the bed when I felt like we were being watched. His eyes widened, and I froze as the same feeling I'd had earlier crept up my legs. The door slammed so hard, the wood trembled. The cabinet next to me slid across the floor, stopping inches from me.

"Bernie, what's happening?" I said, trying to get my legs to move.

"You've got to move," he said, hopping up on his feet. "Walk towards me, one step at a time. You can do it, Brynn."

It felt like I was trapped in the quicksand that haunted my dreams when I was growing up. I took a shuddering step forward as Bernie ran to the edge of the bed, hissing. The feeling slowly faded as I got closer to the bed. I reached out for my cat and pulled him into my arms, holding him close.

"Bernie, what on earth is going on here?"

2

*B*ernie's fur was standing on end as I held him close. That he was this worried made me worry even more. While I knew he was more than just a simple cat, I still wasn't clear what he was. Edward Davis, a crusty ghost who preferred to be called Ned, held Bernie in awe, and I was inclined to believe him. What did it mean if Bernie was freaked out? My heart rate sped up.

"We need to leave," he said, reaching a soft paw up to touch my face. "Calm down, Brynn. I wouldn't let anything happen to you. But this... this may be out of my wheelhouse. Let's get out of here and regroup."

I wanted to follow his instructions, but as we walked into the hallway, I spotted a wisp of something that quickly disappeared into another room. What can I say? I'm a slave to curiosity.

"Hold on to that thought, Bern. I need to see if the ghost in the next room will talk. Maybe whoever it is will know more."

Bernie's eyes closed in frustration and he squiggled to get out of my arms before thumping down on the floor.

"Fine, but make it snappy. I don't like this. I need to do some research."

My steps slowed as I considered what that meant. Bernie had a habit of disappearing at home. Did he have some sort of lair where he had his own laptop? I glanced down at him as I put my hand on the doorknob. His whiskers quirked as he looked up at me.

"Don't even think about asking that. I have my secrets," he said.

I grumbled under my breath as I opened the door and slowly pushed it open. After what happened in the other room, I wasn't too keen on rushing in unprepared. I peeked my head around the corner while Bernie marched in and hopped on the bed, settling himself into the puffy duvet. I couldn't help but snort as he immediately started bathing. He may be more than just a cat, but it was times like this when I wasn't so sure.

"Get off that bed, beastie."

I looked to my left and spotted the ghost of a small, irate woman who was currently shaking her transparent finger in Bernie's direction. She was wearing a long calico dress with a matching mobcap, complete with lace trim.

"He doesn't have fleas," I said, suppressing a smile when she startled and turned her wide eyes towards me.

She wavered a little around the edges and I put my hand up to reassure her. Now that I'd finally contacted a ghost, the last thing I needed was to spook her and have her run off.

"It's okay. I can see you. I'm not here to hurt you."

Her form strengthened, and she folded her substantial arms across her chest and looked me up and down.

"As if you could, missy. What is going on?"

"I was actually hoping you could tell me that. The manager, Russ, asked me to come here and investigate some strange things that have been happening. Do you know anything about that?"

She snorted and eyed Bernie again, shaking her head.

"Shoo, I say. When I was the housekeeper here, we never allowed cats on beds, and I will not start now."

Bernie finally finished his ablutions, lowered his back foot, and fixed his emerald eyes on the incensed ghost.

"I'm not just a cat," he said.

Her eyes bugged out of her head as she looked at us. I needed to act quickly before she vaporized, either out of self preservation or sheer indignation.

"He's not lying. And I wasn't kidding. He doesn't have fleas. We're here to help, but I'm not precisely sure what we're dealing with," I said, taking a deep breath. "I think we got off on the wrong foot. My name's Brynn and this is Bernie. What's your name?"

She looked at me, but her eyes kept straying towards the bed as Bernie went back to his bath.

"Bessie. It's short for Elizabeth, but I like to keep it simple."

"And you were the housekeeper here?"

She straightened her back and nodded her head proudly.

"I was. I was hired shortly after the house was built, back when the family owned the place. I worked here until I was seventy-eight."

I joined Bernie on the bed and stroked his fur as I smiled at the ghost, doing some mental gymnastics in my head to figure out when she'd passed. She'd been a ghost for a long time, which explained her ability to manifest for as long as she had. Even though I was dying to question her about the origins of the house and how she'd ended up spending her afterlife to date here, I needed to find out what was going on.

"That's amazing. How many, um, residents are here?"

Some ghosts don't enjoy talking about themselves as spirits, and gauging from her previous reactions. I didn't want to upset her anymore than we already had.

"There are five of us," she said, with a loud sniff. "We run a tight ship. This place has special meaning for all of us, and we do our part. The tourists expect a good show, and that's what we get. We do not, however, allow animals on the furniture."

Bernie heaved a sigh and hopped down from the bed to sit at her feet. He leveled his patented sweet cat face in her direction and I hid my smile as she softened towards him.

"Even if they are very handsome," she said.

"When we got here and just a few minutes ago, I noticed something strange," I said, deciding I couldn't risk having her lose her hold on her manifestation. "I felt like I'd been frozen in place and this awful feeling of dread came over me."

Her wide face darkened and she took a step back as she raised her hands. The brim of her frilly cap trembled, and she looked from side to side.

"I don't want any part of that. I don't know what it is, and I don't want to know. If you're here to get rid of it, just be done with it. I don't know how much more of it we can take."

She was becoming more translucent by the second, and my mind raced to come up with the right question before she disappeared entirely.

"What changed? When did you first notice it?"

Bessie frowned and shook her head.

"I don't know. Time is different in our place. Besides, weren't you hired to figure this out? Why are you asking me? I've got enough to do around here without doing your job, too."

She had a point, but I literally had nothing to go on.

"What do you have to do?"

She snorted again and faded so much I could barely see her.

"I told you there were five of us. Well, the other four are quality and can't be troubled to take care of themselves. It's up to old Bessie to make sure they're well cared for. Whatever is going on, figure it out, girl. We have little time."

My shoulders slumped as she disappeared. Bernie immediately hopped back on the bed and looked at me, his little face somber.

"We should go. I have a feeling whatever you ran into before is regathering its energy."

I scooped him up, more for my benefit than his, and stroked his soft fur as I walked out of the room. As usual, I had way more questions than answers. I headed down the long hallway and froze as I heard footsteps coming up the stairs. The little hairs on my arms stood up as I listened to the steps get closer.

"Are you done up here? I'm sorry to rush you, but I really need to leave," Norma said.

I let out a breath, feeling foolish for being so paranoid. I pasted a smile on my face as Bernie jumped down and faded into the shadows of the hall.

"I'm just leaving now. I'm sorry to have kept you. I must have lost track of time."

Norma waved me down the stairs in front of her. My senses were on high alert as I walked back down to the lobby. I wasn't in any hurry to experience that freezing dread again. Luckily, I sensed nothing in the open area. The setting sun lit up the interior with a warm glow, and dust motes gave the room an almost ethereal quality. I turned back to Norma, spotting Bernie as he rushed past her and headed for the door.

"Don't worry about it, dear. Oh, here," she said, handing me a business card. "Russ asked me to give this to you."

I flipped it over and saw four digits on the back. This must be the code to the door. I slid it into my pocket, suddenly doubting whether it was smart to come back here at night. I nodded to Norma and headed towards the door, bracing a little as I got closer to it. Bernie's warning really had me spooked, but I went through the door without an issue and felt a little silly as I stood on the porch.

Bernie was waiting at my car, shifting impatiently from foot to foot as I approached. Once I had my door open, he was inside like a shot, sitting upright in the passenger seat. I started the car and pulled onto the street, trying to make sense of everything that had happened.

"Well, at least we didn't run into... whatever that thing is, again," I said, glancing down at him.

Bernie looked out the window and gave a little kitty shrug.

"We haven't seen the last of that. I have a feeling that we're going to see a lot more of it before this is all over."

My stomach twisted itself into a knot at his words and I grimaced as I got onto the highway to head for home. I knew in my heart he was right, but I didn't want to think about the implications of that. Not yet, anyway. I turned on the radio, hoping for some musical distraction as I drove. My boyfriend, Zane Matthews, was due to meet us at my home for dinner.

A little zip worked its way through my chest at the thought of Zane. I'd met the handsome security expert a few months ago, on a job I'd been working on for Bob Tremaine. While we'd gotten off to a rocky start, love had bloomed when I'd least expected it. Growing up in a small town, where I was commonly referred to as the 'ghost girl,' had been tragic for my love life. Meeting him, and having him embrace my gifts, had played a huge role in helping me embrace them as well.

"You're thinking about Zane again, aren't you?" Bernie asked, whiskers quirked.

"Maybe," I said, glancing at him again. "How did you know?"

"You get this look on your face when you're thinking of him. It's cute, but borderline schmaltzy."

I laughed as I shook my head. He was probably right. I'd fallen head over the heels for Zane.

"Hey, can I help it if he's a great guy?" I asked.

Bernie stretched and fluffed out his fur.

"No, he does all that on his own. I'm happy for you, Brynn. You've come a long way, and I think Zane has played a big part in that. You're good for each other."

I blushed at his rare compliment and tried to focus on the road.

"What would you like for supper?"

He settled into a comfortable ball on the seat before answering.

"The answer to that question will always be salmon. But I'll have some of whatever you're having, as well."

"You definitely deserve salmon, bud," I said, ruffling his fur. "We'll see about the rest."

The fading sun cast a glow on the neighboring hills, and the residual fear I'd been feeling since my encounter with whatever that was at the Maddison House faded. Right now, I was looking forward to seeing Zane and figuring out what we were going to do next.

3

*W*e'd only been home long enough for me to let Bernie out of his carrier and dish his food when I heard Zane's Jeep in front of my house. I walked onto the porch to greet him and shivered when the wind hit me. It was definitely the start of hoodie season. I grinned as I saw Zane approaching, laden with takeout bags from our favorite Chinese restaurant.

"You know the way to my heart, don't you?" I said, meeting him on the sidewalk to help.

"I know you love to try new things, so I got a little of everything I thought you'd like," he said before leaning over and kissing my cheek.

"My hero. How was your day?"

He sighed as we walked in the door and dropped our haul on the kitchen table. Bernie appeared, tail held high, and rubbed against Zane's leg.

"Hey, Bernie. Did you take good care of your mom today?" Zane asked, kneeling so he could scratch Bernie's chin. "It was a long day. I think I've got a new client, but I'm not sure."

It was a shame Zane couldn't understand Bernie like I could, but then again, given my cat's questionable sense of humor, that might have been a good thing. I walked into the kitchen to grab some plates and looked across the island as Zane straightened. He ran his fingers through his longish black hair and tried to smile as he noticed me watching him. His icy blue eyes looked tired.

"What do you mean, you're not sure?"

"It's complicated. How was your day?"

"Complicated," I said, sticking my tongue out. "Let's eat and then we can talk about it."

"That sounds like a plan."

I wiggled in my chair as I spooned out my favorite beef and broccoli onto some rice. I like to try new things, but I always start with something I really like. Zane took a huge bite of his shrimp toast, and I suppressed a laugh as Bernie jumped on the chair next to him and put on the most convincing starving cat routine I'd ever seen.

"He just ate," I said, winking as Bernie shot me a glare.

"It's hard work keeping you safe," Bernie said, sniffing. "I need more calories."

Zane buckled and gave Bernie a small piece of ground shrimp, much to my cat's delight, especially given the loud slurping noises he was making.

"Now you're his hero, too," I said, searching for the next container. "What's in this one?"

Zane leaned over and peered into the container.

"Not sure, but it looks like chicken. Or pork."

"Only one way to find out."

I spooned a little onto my rice and took a tentative bite. Oooh, it was twice-cooked pork. I closed my eyes in bliss as the spicy flavors ignited on my tongue. This was simply too good.

"From the sounds you're making, I'm guessing that's a good one. Let me try."

We spent the rest of our meal sampling everything he'd brought, and by the time we were done, I was stuffed. There was still plenty of food left, which meant I had meals for a few days. Score!

Zane helped me clean everything up and we wandered over to my couch to digest and watch some television. He started rubbing my shoulders and I couldn't help but groan as his thumbs got to work.

"Wow, whatever your complicated day entailed, it sure made you tense," he said.

"You go first," I said, stretching my neck to the side.

"Well, like I said, I think I have a new client. He's a software developer from California who's moving to a house in Creekside. He hasn't closed on the place yet, but he had me meet him there. It's a total gut job, so I referred Logan to him to do the work."

Logan was my cousin, although we acted more like siblings. He was a few months older than me, and never let me forget it. When our dads retired, he took over the family construction business, and it was thriving.

"I'm sure Logan will appreciate that. What was the house like?"

"You'd love it. It's on the street right next to Main, you know the one."

"Oh, the Victorian row? You're serious?"

I forgot my massage and turned to face him. Those were my absolute favorite homes in Creekside, although I'd never been able to get inside. Zane chuckled and went back to rubbing my back.

"I am. I also referred you to handle the interior design once Logan's done with the remodel. He said he'd call you in a few days."

"You're the best. Oh, I can't wait to get in there," I said, as visions of tackling another period house danced in my head.

Zane's fingers slowed, and I tilted my head to the side to look at him. His handsome face looked conflicted, and I sensed there was something more to the story.

"What aren't you saying?" I asked. "I'm guessing he wants a security system, but what's wrong?"

"I wouldn't say anything was wrong, but it's just a weird job. He wants a security system, but it's overkill. I honestly couldn't figure out what this guy is so worried about. I don't like to call people paranoid, but wow. I've lived in New York City and have never seen a system like he described. It's like he's preparing for the next world war. I mean, this is South Dakota, for crying out loud. I don't think it's necessary to go that far."

"Are we talking like lasers and stuff here?"

Zane chuckled as he went back to rubbing my back. I listened as he detailed what his client was looking for and ended up shaking my head as he finished the laundry list of security items.

"Wow. Is he a prepper? Or is he more of the zombie apocalypse type?" I asked, dumfounded.

"Zombies aren't real. Wait, are they?"

Zane, while accepting of ghosts, was still new to the paranormal world I was getting more comfortable with. That was the main reason I was stalling about telling him about my day. I turned to face him and shook my head.

"I don't think they're real."

"They're real alright," Bernie announced as he joined us on the couch and got comfortable. "They're not what you think, but they're real."

Zane looked between us and cocked an eyebrow.

"What did he just say?"

"Um, he said they're real, but not what we think. I don't think I want to know any more about that tonight. I'd like to sleep well."

Zane placed a kiss on my forehead.

"That makes two of us. So, that was my day. The job is mine if I want it, but I don't know if I do."

"It sounds like he's not afraid to pay for what he wants. What's the harm if it makes him feel safe? I mean, he is coming from California. Maybe he's used to living in an area with a lot higher crime rate."

Zane shrugged before wrapping a muscular arm around my shoulders.

"You have a point. How about your day? I've learned when you say complicated, you mean it."

I debated on whether I wanted to tell him about the Maddison House. We'd gotten to where we weren't keeping anything back, but I wasn't sure how much detail I wanted to go into.

"Well... I don't really know what we're dealing with, but it was... it was different."

Bernie's ears swiveled in my direction as I talked about what we'd seen and felt while we were at the museum. Zane's eyes flew open wide as I talked, and he straightened a little.

"So, what do you think you're dealing with? A furious ghost? Is this like the banshee at the hotel?"

Bernie mumbled a word that sounded very much like what I didn't want to hear, but I had a sinking feeling he was right. I wasn't ready to accept it, but it would not surprise me if he was correct.

"Maybe. I need to do some research before I can say for sure. Russ is so nice. You'd really like him. And the house. Maybe you can come with me sometime," I said, trailing off as I realized that might not be the best idea.

"I'd love that. So, you're going to do the job?"

I nodded and glanced at Bernie, who was now sleeping like the world's most innocent cat.

"I think so. I'm curious to see what's really going on. I can't help it."

Zane nodded and chucked me under the chin gently.

"That's my girl. I think you're the most curious person I've ever met."

"And that's a good thing, right?"

Even though I knew Zane supported me and accepted my strange abilities, there was a small part of me that still expected he'd learn something that would send him right out the door and out of my life. It was something I was working on, but hey, I'm not perfect.

His blue eyes met mine, and he smiled before kissing me softly.

"It's a perfect thing. I love that about you."

My cheeks heated as I felt a blush work its way up my neck onto my face. Coupled with my vibrant red hair, I knew I probably looked like a very ripe tomato, but it was hard to care after a kiss like that. I snuggled into his side and watched as he flipped through the channels, settling on a game of football. My eyes were heavy, and I felt myself drifting off in his warm embrace.

The next thing I knew, I opened my eyes into a misty landscape that was eerily familiar. My heart sped up as I looked around, trying to see. This had to be the ether, a place I didn't quite understand, but had visited more than once. Typically, when I woke up here, Bernie was waiting for me. In fact, it had been the first place I'd actually been able to hear his voice.

I looked around, hoping to spot his furry behind and tell him to get us out of here, but he was nowhere to be found. This was... odd. A strange sound caught my attention, and I turned in the direction I thought it was coming from. It was an eerie howl. The hair on the back of my neck stood up as it got louder and I swallowed hard, mouth dry. I felt frozen in place, much like I had earlier, but somehow, my body was moving against my will.

I tried to scream, but it was like my jaw was wired shut. No sound would come out, despite my best efforts. An icy chill worked its way down my spine, and it felt like my bones would crack as I tried to resist. A whisper sounded to my left, but I couldn't turn my head. It kept repeating itself, getting closer, until it felt like it was right next to me.

"You'll never get away," it hissed. *"You're mine..."*

A scream echoed through the ether, jolting me.

"Brynn! Wake up!"

My eyes flew open, and I realized I was the one screaming as Zane gripped me. Every hair on Bernie's body was standing on end and he looked terrified as he yowled to match me. I snapped my mouth shut and the blood curdling sound stopped. Bernie quieted, but his sides were heaving as our eyes locked.

"I'm so sorry," I said, croaking out the words as I tried to catch my breath.

Zane slowly released me from his grip and sat back so he could see my face. He looked haggard, and my hand automatically went up to stroke his cheek.

"What on earth was that? You fell asleep and then I drifted off, and the next thing I knew, you were stiff as a board and screaming at the top of your lungs."

I leaned my head against his chest and listened to the rapid thumping of his heart as I tried to gather my wits. Bernie walked across Zane's lap to crowd into mine. I stroked his soft fur and took a deep breath to calm myself.

"I don't know. It was like a nightmare, but I was in that place Bernie calls the ether. I couldn't move and there was this strange music playing. Someone said I could never get away and I think that's when I started screaming. I'm so sorry."

He brushed my hair off my face and stroked my head as I lay against his chest.

"You scared the living s... stuffing out of me. Are you okay?"

I nodded, embarrassed.

"I'm fine. It was just a bad dream."

I could feel his disbelief wafting off of him, but this was an argument I was not willing to get into. Not tonight. I felt his heart rate slow and mine echoed it as I relaxed.

"I don't think it was just a dream, but I don't want to fight about it. I also don't want to leave you alone tonight. Is it okay if I stay? I don't feel right leaving you. No funny business."

I reluctantly straightened so I could see him, and my heart warmed at his gentle tone and the look on his face. While romance was the furthest thing from my mind tonight, I knew I'd appreciate his presence. I wasn't sure I wanted to go to sleep again, but having him here made me feel much safer.

"I'd like that. I'm sure I'll be fine, but if you want to stay, you're more than welcome."

He pulled me back into his arms and rested his head on the top of mine.

"Let's watch some more television and relax. If it happens again, I'm here, baby. I'll follow you anywhere to protect you, even into your dreams."

I let out a deep breath as I got comfortable. This night wasn't turning out how I'd envisioned it, but right now, with a warm cat on my lap and an incredible man at my side, I couldn't knock it. I intentionally cleared my head of the busy thoughts that were tumbling around and tried to focus on the game. Tomorrow would be soon enough to figure out what was happening.

4

*T*he morning came quicker than I would have liked, but as I lay snuggled in bed with Zane on my left and Bernie on my right, I couldn't knock it too much. I didn't want to be a creeper, but I couldn't resist looking at Zane's face as he slept. His chiseled face was relaxed, and a slight smile turned the corners of his lips up.

"You've got it bad, don't you?" Bernie asked as he sat up and stretched.

"I do, cat."

"I approve. Even though I usually like to sleep on that side, it was comforting he was here."

"I know, right?"

Zane's eyelids flickered, and he smiled as he noticed the two of us staring at him.

"Good morning, you two. How long have you been watching me sleep?"

"What answer doesn't appear too creepy?"

"Anything less than two minutes is fine. Five would push it."

"Two it is," I said, flashing him a cheeky grin. "Did you sleep well?"

He rubbed his hands over his face before stretching out his arms.

"I did. I'm more worried about how you slept, though."

He rolled over and stroked my hair, tucking it behind my ear. I'd forgotten to braid it, and I didn't need a mirror to guess how bad the tangles were going to be.

"I slept like a baby."

Zane kissed my cheek and Bernie gave me a smirk before hopping off the bed and padding to the kitchen.

"He's going to want his food," I said, reluctantly pulling away. "Can I make you some breakfast, too?"

Zane threw off the covers and held out his hand to pull me up.

"How about I make breakfast?"

"You are a prince among men."

I made a show out of slapping his rear before padding into the bathroom to brush my teeth. I said a silent thank you that Zane had gone for a kiss on the cheek instead of my mouth. Whew.

As I got ready, I thought about the build-up I'd made in my mind about Zane staying the night. All we'd done was cuddle, but I was surprised we hadn't felt awkward. I tossed a hoodie over my tee shirt and headed towards the kitchen, following my nose towards the delicious scents.

"What is this?"

As I came around the corner, I spotted Bernie happily tucking into his breakfast while Zane was busy at the stove. I peeked over his shoulder while he tried to block my view of the pan.

"It's a surprise. I know how much you like French toast, and since all I could find were eggs, bread and milk, it seemed perfect. The coffee should be ready."

I grabbed two mugs and poured us both a cup of the steaming brew. It smelled better than ever, and I cocked an eyebrow as I took my first sip.

"Why does this taste so good?"

Zane flipped the bread over before leaning close to kiss me on the nose.

"Because it was made with love. I hope Bernie approves of the food I picked for him. I even remembered to feed him before I made the coffee."

"Ah yes, the cat before coffee rule. Seriously, though, Zane, thank you. This is wonderful. You didn't need to go to all of this trouble. A piece of toast would have been fine."

"You're my girl and I'm going to spoil you. Oh shoot, I forgot to check for syrup. Do you have any?"

I bit my lip as I started searching through my cupboards. I rarely made breakfast, and any syrup I had was bound to be old. Syrup never spoils, does it? I certainly hope not. My fingers latched on a sticky bottle and I let out a shout as I pulled it from the cupboard.

"Yes! I have syrup," I said, washing off my fingers in the sink.

"Perfect. Your breakfast is served, my dear," he said, bowing with a flourish.

"You're the best."

He twirled the spatula like it was a gun and put two more pieces of French toast into the pan.

"Eat," he said, edging the bread around. "I don't want yours to get cold. It's my secret recipe."

I took an appreciative sniff and looked back at him.

"Cinnamon?"

He nodded, eyes crinkled as he flipped his toast.

"How did you guess?"

"My mom used to make it this way. I'll wait for you since yours is almost done."

We devoured our breakfast in record time, and it was delicious, even with the ancient syrup. Bernie hopped on the table as I finished up and did a quick rendition of his starving cat routine as I dredged my last forkful through the syrup.

"I don't think cats can have sweets like this," I said, pausing as I raised my fork to my mouth.

"It will be fine," Bernie said, eyes huge. "Just a tiny bite for a starving cat. You can spare that, can't you?"

I rolled my eyes as I broke off a tiny piece and handed it over. This cat had me wrapped around his paw.

"I literally just watched you slay an entire can of salmon. Somehow I don't buy that you're hungry."

His eyes gleamed as he licked at his treat before swallowing it whole. He switched his attention to Zane, who'd luckily cleaned his plate in the interim.

"Sorry, bud," Zane said, ruffling Bernie's fur. "All gone."

My cat sniffed before regally jumping off the table and stalking towards the living room.

"Thanks for making this," I said, grabbing his plate and heading for the dishwasher. "It was amazing."

"I'm glad you liked it. What are your plans for the day?"

I rinsed the dishes before putting them in the machine and leaned against the counter to look at him.

"I need more information, so I think I'll head to the library. How about you?"

"Tell Sophie hi for me. I've got a few things to do in Creekside and then I'll head back up here. Would you like to have dinner together?"

"Always. But maybe I should go to your house instead. I feel guilty that we always end up here."

He leaned in close and wrapped his arms around my waist, pulling me close, before putting his forehead against mine.

"I love your house. My rental is tiny and I think the landlord would have a stroke if he saw Bernie. I don't mind coming up here. Besides, I want to know what you find out today."

"Are you talking to that potential client again?"

Zane stepped back and grimaced as he tucked a piece of his hair behind an ear.

"We'll see. I'm still not sure what to think of that job. It pays well, though. I'd better head out so I can get ready for the day."

"You know, you might bring a few things tonight," I said, blushing and staring at my feet. "So you don't have to leave."

Zane tipped my chin up so I could look at him, and what I saw in those icy blue eyes took my breath away.

"You mean it?"

I nodded, not trusting my voice. His eyes crinkled as he grinned at me and moved back in for a quick kiss.

"I'll do that. Don't be afraid to text me during the day. I don't have that much going on."

"I will. Thanks for staying. It... well, it meant a lot."

"Always," he said. "If I'd left, I would have worried about you all night. At least I could watch you."

"It wasn't for over five minutes, was it?" I asked, teasing.

"No, it was definitely under two. See you later, Sullivan."

I watched him walk down the sidewalk for a few seconds before I answered.

"Later, Matthews."

I shut the door and headed for the living room to find my cat. He was sunning on the sofa, ebony fur glistening in the morning light.

"Ready to go, buddy?"

He gave his immaculate coat one last lick before jumping down and heading for the carrier I kept near the door.

"I thought you'd never ask."

"Hey, the library doesn't open until nine, so it's not like we were in a hurry."

He let out a kitty huff as I couldn't help but giggle a little as I carried him to my car. I felt giddy and ready to take on anything. I turned up the music and sang along as I drove to Deadwood.

By the time I pulled to a stop in front of the library, I'd almost put my awful nightmare out of my mind. Almost. I grabbed Bernie's bag and headed for the front door. Even though animals weren't technically allowed in the library, my friend, and head librarian, Sophie Ryman, made an exception for Bernie. I breezed through the doors and immediately spotted my bohemian friend behind the front desk. She clapped her hands together when she saw us, jingling the many bracelets she wore on her wrists.

"Brynn! It's so good to see you again. Hello, you handsome cat," she said, booping Bernie's nose through the mesh of his bag. "Stacia is off today, so I'm here by my lonesome. What brings you here on this crisp autumn morning?"

I couldn't help but grin as Sophie wrapped me in a warm embrace. I'd known her since I was a child, and she'd become an honorary aunt of sorts. I appreciated she knew about my abilities and never made me feel uncomfortable about it. In fact, she delighted in learning more and was an incredible researcher.

"I've got a fresh case that I think might interest you," I said, shifting Bernie's bag off my shoulder and rolling it.

"I'm all ears."

"You know the Maddison House, right?"

"Of course. It's a delightful place. I always hope I'll spot something paranormal when I visit, but alas, I never have. What's happening there?"

I leaned my hip against the desk as I filled Sophie in on everything that had happened the day before. Her eyes grew bigger as she listened, and by the time I was done, she looked as concerned as I felt.

"Oh dear, that doesn't sound good," she said, tapping her finger on her lip. "Do you think it might be a poltergeist?"

There it was. The word I'd been avoiding like the plague. In all my years of seeing and communicating with ghosts, I'd yet to run into one, and it wasn't high on my must-do list, if you know what I mean. So far, my experience with them was entirely limited to the creepy movies that came out when I was little. I'd never been able to watch one all the way through, and there was absolutely no chance I was going to start now.

"I hope not. If that's the case, I'm in way over my head."

She patted my arm and gave me a serious look.

"Whatever it is, Brynn, I'll know you'll meet it head on and do what needs to be done. You're gifted, my dear."

"I don't know about that, but whatever it is, I need to help the other ghosts who live in that house. I've never heard of anything like this, but something definitely needs to be done. I was hoping to research more of the history of the house and see what I can learn."

I grabbed Bernie's bag and slung it back over my shoulder. Someone needed to go a little lighter on the salmon, judging from the

THE ETHER IN THE ENTRYWAY

weight of the bag. Sophie tucked her arm in mine and led me back to the Dakota room, where all of our local history was concentrated.

"Now that's something I can help you with. I may need to nip back out to the front if someone else comes in, but mornings are usually pretty slow. Let's see what we can find out."

Sophie bustled around the room while I got Bernie settled on top of the table. I couldn't let him out, but it felt right having him close while I researched. She bustled back to the table, laden with several books, and plunked them down on the table.

"I'll let you start with the house, and I'll head to the paranormal section. Even if you don't think that's what we're dealing with, it wouldn't hurt to do a little research, just in case."

I gave her a weak smile while visions of slamming cupboards and horrible noises danced in my head. I shook off the feeling of dread and cracked open the first book on the pile, hoping to find some answers.

5

*A*fter several hours of research, I learned a lot more about the house and its transition into a museum, but I still wasn't certain I wanted to embrace the whole poltergeist angle. I brushed my hands over the cover of the book Sophie left while she helped another patron and sighed.

"If it is a poltergeist, we'll deal with it," Bernie said, his voice soft.

"I know. I just don't know. It freaks me out. I need to learn more about them, but I feel like I really don't want to know the truth. I mean, if it is, does that mean we need to get in touch with a local priest or something? I'm out of my depth here, bud."

"Brynn, who are you talking to?" Sophie asked as she breezed in.

I hadn't even heard the telltale tinkling of her bracelets as she approached. I jumped a little and flashed her a smile as I considered telling her about my new ability to communicate with my cat. She'd supported me through even stranger revelations, but I held my tongue. Maybe someday I'd tell her, but it wouldn't be today.

"Just running an idea past Bernie. It helps me think. Is it okay if I take a few of these books home? I'd like to read through them when I'm in a little better frame of mind."

Sophie cocked her head to the side and clucked her tongue.

"It's a lot, isn't it? Of course, dear, I'll put them on your account. As busy as you've been, you have had little time to read for pleasure, have you?"

I packed up the book and stood so I could push my chair in. She was absolutely right. I used to live for books, and lately, that had definitely fallen by the wayside.

"You're absolutely right. Do you have any suggestions? I need to make time to read. It might help me decompress."

"I've got just the series for you. I think you'll enjoy it. It's about a girl who can see ghosts," Sophie said, eyes twinkling. "You can see if it's accurate. You know, I've often thought someone should write a book about you and what you've experienced."

I couldn't help but laugh as I grabbed Bernie's bag and followed Sophie to the front desk.

"I don't know about that, but I'm happy to try the series. If you're recommending it, I'm sure it must be good."

"We'll see what you think. There are about six books out, so you'll have plenty to go through if you like it."

She scanned the books and handed me a paperback. I glanced at the cover, smiling as I saw it featured a girl and her cat.

"Hey, she's got a cat, too."

Sophie winked as I slid the book into my bag.

"I'll do a little research on my own and see what I can come up with. Please keep me updated, dear. You know how much I love hearing about your cases. I've got a few other paranormal books I'd like to go through."

"Thanks, Sophie. You're the best, brightest, and..."

"Boisterous?" she answered, completing our ritual game.

"I was going to say beautiful, but I like it," I said, laughing as I folded her into a hug. "See you soon."

I walked out into the sunshine and glanced at my phone's screen to check the time. It was almost lunchtime, and my breakfast had long since worn off. I tapped on my phone and pulled up Logan's number.

"Hey, carrot cake. What's up?"

I rolled my eyes as I walked. My cousin made a game of coming up with horrible nicknames for me, but that one was bad. Back in high school, the local kids had bullied me pretty severely, not only for my blazing red hair but also my ability to see ghosts. Somehow, when he said the names, it didn't hurt as much, and in fact, had made me almost immune to teasing.

"I think that's the worst one you've ever come up with. I was going to ask if you wanted to meet me for lunch at Jill's, but now I'm not so sure."

He snorted through the phone.

"Whatever. I think that was perfect. I am in town, and I'd love to have you buy my lunch."

"Whoa, there, I said nothing about paying," I said as I slid into my car.

I was kidding, and Logan knew it. I blew a raspberry into the phone as he laughed at me. What can I say? We weren't the most mature adults on a good day, and that was okay. Logan had been there for me through some very rough times, and even though he irritated me to no end, he still was the brother I'd never had.

"I can be there in five minutes."

"See you there."

I ended the call and started my car, glancing over at Bernie in the passenger seat. I already knew what he was thinking and held up my hand to forestall his typical routine.

"I'll save you something. Are you okay hanging out in the car while Logan and I have lunch?"

"I guess," he said, sniffing hard. "Don't forget to roll down a window so I don't suffocate."

He slowly blinked his beautiful green eyes to let me know he was teasing and huffed a little kitty laugh before stretching.

"We wouldn't want that," I said, coming to a stop in front of my favorite diner. "I shouldn't be too long and I'll make it worth your wait."

Jill's Cafe was one of my favorite spots to eat in Deadwood. It was the place where my father would take me for special lunches when I was a kid, and I loved the fifties vibe. The owner, Jill, wore poodle skirts and twin sets, further completing the illusion that you'd stepped back in time to a simpler place. My mouth started watering as I envisioned the classic bacon cheeseburger and fries I always ordered.

Logan pulled up behind me in his pickup and gave me a cheery wave as I got out.

"I thought you would have had lunch with your love muffin," he said, falling in next to me as we walked towards the entrance.

"Ew, love muffin? The 90s called. They want their corny sayings back."

"That's a classic, and don't you forget it. Speaking of your love muffin, how is Zane?"

"He's great. We had dinner last night. How's Kelsie?"

Kelsie, Logan's girlfriend, had been one of the mean girls in our high school, but we'd all changed, and she surprised me with her new attitude. When they'd first gotten together, I wasn't sure how I'd felt about it, but now? She was probably one of the best things that ever happened to my cousin. He was known for being the loving and leaving type, but so far, he'd really focused on her, something that made me very glad.

"She's great. We had dinner, too."

"Awwww," I said, waving to Jill as I found a booth.

She bustled in our direction, giving me a broad smile before leaning against the corner of the booth.

"What'll it be today, kids?"

I didn't even need to look at the menu.

"I'll have a bacon cheeseburger and a Coke. Where's Dave?"

A tinge of red flooded her cheeks and my inner matchmaker did a little happy dance. I'd given Jill, and Dave Beldon, the local sheriff, a much needed push in each other's direction a few months ago, and they were the cutest couple.

"He's supposed to be in later. He said he got tied up with some sort of disturbance."

"I hope it isn't serious," I said, glancing at Logan as he looked over the menu. "What are you having? My treat, so go hog wild."

Logan cocked an eyebrow and gave me a crooked smile as he tapped his finger on his lip.

"In that case, I'll have the prime rib and crab legs."

Jill flicked the dishtowel from her shoulder in Logan's direction and rolled her eyes.

"You know dang well we don't serve that high-faluting stuff here. You'll have the patty melt. Back in a flash."

"How did she know that's what I wanted?" Logan asked, settling back into the booth.

"She always does. I swear she can read minds. What do you think is going on with that disturbance?"

Deadwood was a small town, and although it was a tourist destination, we rarely had too many issues with crime. Well, other than the rash of murders that had taken place in the past few months, but I overlooked that.

Logan shrugged and drummed his fingers on the table.

"Not sure. So, what did you want to talk about?"

"How do you know I wanted to talk? Maybe I just wanted the company of my favorite cousin while we enjoyed a pleasant lunch?"

"I'm your only cousin."

"True, my selection small of favorites is quite small," I said, sticking my tongue out at him. "Anyway, I don't want to bore you with work talk. What have you been up to?"

"Spill it, Brynnie. I can tell something is bothering you. My fantastic tales of renovations can wait for a few minutes."

I took a deep breath before launching into my tale. Logan's eyebrows looked like they wanted to fly off his face as he listened. By the time I was done, our food arrived, and I was immediately distracted by the delicious smells coming from my plate.

"This looks so good," I said, jamming a fry into my mouth.

"You're so ladylike," Logan said. "No wonder Zane is crazy about you."

I took a giant bite of my burger while I narrowed my eyes at him, making him laugh as he examined his patty melt. I nipped off a small piece of burger to put aside for Bernie.

"How is this always so good?" he asked, taking a huge bite of his own.

"Obviously, our eating habits run in the family."

"That's the only thing that runs," he said with his mouth full,

We focused on our meals, and I'd cleaned my plate by the time Dave Beldon walked in. He looked tired as he stopped at our booth and I motioned for Logan to scoot over so he could join us. Dave took off his cowboy hat and let out a groan as I snagged a fry from Logan's plate, hoping he wouldn't notice.

"Hey, I saw that!"

Whoops. I chomped on the fry and turned to Dave.

"Jill said you were dealing with a disturbance. Is everything okay?"

He scratched his head and nodded slowly, smiling as Jill approached.

"Hey, pumpkin," he said, blushing as he noticed Logan and me staring at him. "I'll have the patty melt."

Jill put a hand on his shoulder and squeezed gently as she searched his face. She glanced at me before heading back to the kitchen to put in his order. Dave fixed me with an interesting look and leaned back in the booth.

"Do you know anything about a group called the Ghost Twins?"

"The what now?"

"Is that a cartoon or something?" Logan asked, pivoting in the booth so he could look at Dave's face.

Dave snorted and looked up at the ceiling.

"Well, they're certainly cartoonish. I thought maybe given your, well, what you do, you might have heard about them. From what they were saying, they've got a popular television show where they hunt ghosts. It's two brothers and a film crew."

Understanding dawned, and I shook my head.

"I get it. I don't watch those shows, but I know what you're talking about. They're here? In Deadwood?"

"Yes, ma'am. They've set up camp outside the Maddison House and they're demanding entrance in the name of public safety."

"Can they do that?"

Dave shook his head as he made eye contact.

"The Maddison House is private property, so technically, no. They didn't want to hear that, though. It took everything my deputies had to escort them off the scene. They made a bunch of noise about gaining access. Do you know what's going on?"

I bit my lip and looked over at Logan for backup. Dave was aware of what I could do. In fact, I'd helped him solve a cold case when I was a teenager. He wasn't exactly comfortable with it, but he trusted me. Lately, we'd been thrown together in several cases, and I knew he was reaching a point where he couldn't deny a belief in the paranormal.

"Well, there are a few odd things going on. I spoke with the manager, Russ, yesterday about it. They want to hire me to investigate. I can't say for certain what's happening yet, but he mentioned they were getting some critical reviews online. Maybe the wonder twins read it there."

"Ghost Twins," Dave said, correcting me with a smirk.

"Meh, I like wonder twins better. Maybe they fist bump each other to get more powers."

Logan started laughing, and the mood at the table eased. Jill joined us, sliding a plate in front of Dave, before plopping into the booth next to me.

"Do you think they're legit?" Logan asked.

Dave picked up a fry and studied my face before shaking his head.

"No. I don't. This one here," he said, gesturing with his fry. "She's the real deal. I think these guys are phonies. With any luck, they'll take a hint and get out of town. I don't think we'll have to worry about it."

My uneasy stomach wasn't so sure. I pasted on a smile and tried to be positive.

"Well, we'll hope for the best. Having a team of people running around would definitely make my job harder."

"Do I even want to know what we're talking about?" Jill asked.

"Probably not. Thanks for the patty melt," Dave said, giving her a special smile that left her cheeks red.

As much as I wanted to stay and indulge my cheering inner matchmaker, I needed to get back to researching what was going on at the museum. I wanted to be fully armed with facts when I revisited the Maddison House.

"Lunch was delicious, as always," I said, grabbing the napkin with Bernie's treats and my bag. "I've got the bill."

"Nonsense. Today's on the house, kids," Jill said, sliding out so I could stand.

"Whatever," Logan said. "Brynn never buys lunch, and I'm not robbing her of the opportunity."

Dave let Logan out of the booth and I spotted Jill's helper, Kelly, up at the register.

"I'll take care of this. See you two later," I said, as Jill sat back down.

I paid the check and left a tip for Jill before following Logan out onto the street. The breeze was a little chilly, and I tugged my hoodie sleeves down to cover my hands as I walked back to my car.

"What do you have planned for the rest of the day?" Logan asked.

"More research. How about you?"

"I've got to get my crew ready for our next job. Hey, did you ever find a house for those people who worked for the Graffs?"

My last case had involved a richer than rich local family. The patriarch of the family passed on, and his will left his butler without a place to leave. One of the last things Mr. Graff had done was pay me a whopping fifty thousand dollars to find his killer, and I wanted to invest the money into a fixer upper to help the butler and his wife.

"We're still looking. Bob said he had a few ideas. Are you still on board to do the renovations?"

"Absolutely. I'll see if I can find anything, too. You know, it wouldn't hurt to look near Coppertown. It's just a few miles away and the homes are a lot more affordable up there."

"Good idea."

"I'm full of them."

"You're full of something," I said, elbowing Logan in the ribs. "Thanks for having lunch with me."

"Any time. Especially when you're buying. Call me and we can do a double date sometime this week."

"Sounds good."

I got into my car and dug in my bag for Bernie's treat while I told him about what I'd learned about the ghost hunting team in town. He stopped chewing long enough to level a look of disdain at me.

"You can't be serious. That rag-tag crew? I thought they were heading to Louisiana."

"Wait, you know about the Ghost Twins?"

"I know things. I also know they're absolutely full of it. We'll want to give them a wide berth. The last thing you need is to have someone capture what you can do on camera. You'd get no rest."

"That's the last thing I want. What do you think we should do for the rest of the day?"

"About that," Bernie said, swiping a paw over his muzzle. "I think we need to go visit an old friend. He might have some answers for us. Thanks for the burger, by the way. It was delicious."

"Great. What do you mean, old friend?"

"We need to go back up the mountain and talk to Ned."

"Oh no. Are you serious?"

He nodded slowly.

"Right now, it's our best option. Ned is much more than he seems. I strongly feel he has some answers."

I started the engine and bit back a curse. Ned was possibly the last person, well, ghost, I wanted to see today. He was the spirit of an old miner who'd been around so long he'd developed the ability to manipulate the physical environment. He'd helped me talk to Bernie, but that didn't mean I trusted him completely. I'd offered to help him move on, but he wasn't interested, preferring to keep scaring people who rented cabins at the resort. I steered my car onto the highway and headed for the mountain resort where we'd last seen him. This day just kept getting stranger.

6

*W*e pulled to a stop in front of the rental cabin where I'd last seen Ned Davis, and I turned off the engine. Luckily, the cabin looked vacant, so I wouldn't have to worry about being spotted. I felt a shiver work its way through my spine as I remembered what happened at this place a few months ago.

An innocent man had been murdered, and my cousin was nearly killed by the unhinged person who'd committed the crime. At first, we'd thought Ned was the one who killed the man, but it didn't take long to learn that although he was definitely a different ghost, he wasn't murderous. Well, at least I hoped not.

"Bernie, do you think he's around?" I asked as I opened the door.

He flew past me and stretched once he was on the ground.

"How do I know? I'm not a magical Ned detector. It makes sense, though. This place was built on his old claim. I'm guessing it's at least possible he'll be here."

Bernie stalked towards the back of the cabin, tail held high, as I followed him.

"You don't need to be so snarky."

He paused, one paw in the air, and looked over his shoulder, blinking slowly.

"Sorry. I've got a lot on my mind. I want to do everything possible to keep you safe, and I'm not sure what we're dealing with."

"And you think Ned will have the answers?"

"He *might* have some answers. That's the best we can hope for."

Well, I guess I'll take it. It's not like we had a ton of options at this point. I kept trudging after my cat until we ended up facing the woods behind the cabin. I couldn't help but look at the spot where the body had been discovered. I shivered again and tried to focus on happier things.

A brief look at the woods made me question the whole happier thing. The trees had lost their leaves, and their bare white bark made the trunks look like bones propped up in a strange formation. Wow, I really needed to find something happy to think about.

Bernie walked forward into the trees and I took a deep breath before following. I enjoy being outdoors and all, but I much prefer being in an old house, working to make it beautiful again. This was a field trip I could do without.

"Bernie, do you think he's here?"

His ear twitched, and I knew he heard me, but he kept pacing forward with a determined step. I guess if a ten-pound cat wasn't scared, I shouldn't be, but then again, he said he was more than just a cat. In fact, Ned was the one who started that whole thing. Before we'd met him, I thought Bernie was a regular, albeit long-lived cat. He'd first arrived with my family when I was a small child, and he was still with me nearly twenty-some years later.

I felt a little silly for not realizing before that it was incredibly rare to have a cat that old, particularly one who never seemed to age, but I hadn't. I stored some new questions in the mental pile I was keeping to ask Bernie whenever he felt like sharing some more information about himself. That hasn't happened yet, but I try to be optimistic.

I felt an icy chill as the breeze picked up and I came to a halt, eyes drawn up to the trees. We were deeper in the forest now, where pine trees ruled, and the wind made a howling noise as it rushed through the needles. Something was here.

Bernie traced his way back to me and sat at my feet, curling his tail across the tops of my boots.

"He's coming. Let me do the talking."

I shrugged, content to let my tiny tyrant order me around. He knew way more about this stuff than I did, apparently, and right now, I wasn't sure what I needed to ask Ned.

My thoughts cut off as a cackle echoed through the tree grove. A dark shape appeared to our left and started lumbering towards us. The first time I'd seen Ned, I'd been convinced I was dealing with some sort of ghost bear, thanks to the bear pelt the ghost still wore. Spirits usually showed up wearing what they had on when they died, and Ned was no exception.

"Hiya, girly. I didn't expect to see you again so soon. I see you have your beast with you."

"Hi, Ned. Scare any campers lately?"

As he got closer, I could see his twisted frame more clearly. He'd had a mining accident that twisted his back and legs before he died, and although most ghosts appeared to be physically fine once they passed, he was an exception. I had a feeling Ned was always going to be the exception to the rule.

"I might have. There was this one girl, oh you should have heard her scream. Ah, that was a good day."

"You shouldn't do that, you know. It's not very nice."

"Oh, there's no harm in scaring people and moving a few things around. You need to relax."

"As much as I'd love to sit here with this delightful conversation, we have questions, Ned. I'm hoping you have answers," Bernie said.

"Mebbe I do, mebbe I don't. What's it to you, cat?"

Bernie's eyes took on a dangerous gleam as the miner's ghost cackled and danced a little jig. He was easily the most incorrigible ghost I'd ever seen, but he'd helped save my cousin's life and made it possible for me to talk to Bernie, so I couldn't be all mad at him.

"Ned, if you could help, that would be great," I said, to soften Bernie's demand. "We're dealing with a weird situation."

Ned zipped closer to me, forcing me to take a step back. It was a good thing that while I could hear and see ghosts, smelling them wasn't an option. It didn't look like Ned had been the cleanest person while he was alive.

"Whaddya mean, weird?"

Bernie's little chest rose and fell in a giant sigh before he quickly told Ned about what we'd seen at the Maddison House. I noticed he didn't mention my dream or whatever it was in the ether, and I was going to add that when he looked at me and shook his head sharply. I shut my mouth with an audible click.

"What's that, girlie? Did you have something to say?"

"Nope. Bernie did a great job summing it up."

"Alrighty. What do you want me to do about it? If you're asking me, and you obviously are, it sounds like it's your problem, not my problem."

He let out another unearthly cackle and zoomed around the clearing. While he irritated me to no end, it made me absurdly happy that he was so mobile. With his back injury, it must have been very difficult to get around when he was alive. I know. I'm a big softie.

"It could very well be your problem, if you know what I mean," Bernie said, eyes narrowed dangerously. "I don't expect you to do anything, but I was hoping you might have some insight given your unique situation."

Ned came to a halt, and he drifted closer to us, eyeing Bernie with dislike.

"You threatening me, kitty cat? I still don't know what you are exactly, but I'm not afraid of you."

I didn't miss the way Ned's eyes flicked from side-to-side. He seemed afraid, or at least respectful, of Bernie. I really needed to get him to tell me what he was.

"I'm not threatening you. I simply thought you might be assist us. If you're unwilling, we'll let you go," Bernie said before rising and stalking past me, tail lashing.

I shrugged and turned to follow him, suppressing a smile as I saw Ned race ahead of us.

"Hey, you just got here. You don't have to run off so fast. I don't get to talk to many people."

My heart went out to the old ghost, and I slowed my steps.

"Ned, my offer to help you cross over still stands. I can't imagine how lonely it is for you out here."

"Whoa, girlie, I said nothing about that," Ned said, raising his hands and backing away. "Just saying it's nice to have a sit down talk with folks every now and again."

Bernie heaved another sigh and walked back over.

"Have you felt any disturbances in the area over the past few months?"

Ned scratched his beard, and I tried not to shudder as I wondered if lice went with a ghost when someone passed. Was there such a thing as ghost lice? I shook off that thought and focused on the ghost.

"Now that you say that, I felt something. I don't know exactly when it was, but there was a ripple."

"What's a ripple?" I asked, looking between the two.

They conveniently ignored me.

"Have you noticed anything else odd since then?"

"Come to mention it, things have been a little off lately. I've seen quite a few others around. I call 'em the soul suckers."

"Others? Soul suckers?" I asked, only to be ignored again.

"Do you manifest elsewhere? I know you can. Are things concentrated in Deadwood?"

"I can, but I haven't lately," Ned said, eyes darting to the side.

Bernie narrowed his eyes and fixed Ned with a ruthless stare. The ghost whirled around and refused to make eye contact.

"Ripple? Others? Soul suckers? Is this on?" I asked, tapping on an imaginary microphone.

"What do you know?" Bernie asked, walking closer to Ned. "I can tell you've seen something."

"Mebbe I have, mebbe I haven't. Old Ned was never a rat and I have no intention of starting now."

"It could be very important," I said, eyes bouncing between the pair. "Please, Ned, if you know something..."

"I'm not saying I do, but I will say something odd happened and things haven't been right since. That's all I've got."

Ned spread his hands wide and blinked out of sight. A gust of wind picked up my hair, tangling it almost instantly. I stifled a curse as I tried to get my fingers through the snarl. Ned was really the worst.

"Well, that's all we're going to get today. Let's go."

"We got very little," I said, panting to keep up with Bernie as he raced through the woods.

"We got enough," he said over his shoulder. "I've got a direction to go in."

"It's not in the P-word direction, is it? I really don't want it to be that."

Bernie came to a halt and looked at me with gentle eyes.

"It's not what you think, Brynn. The movies always distort things. We're not dealing with an evil demon."

"Well, that makes me feel better."

"There is a possibility we're dealing with an unhinged and tortured soul who's trying to change his destination."

Okay, so that made me feel worse.

"Wait, what?"

Bernie continued down the trail, moving fast as he ignored my question. I grumbled as I followed him, muttering under my breath.

"Ripples, others, and now tortured souls. This day is just turning out to be fantastic."

"I heard that," Bernie said.

"I wasn't whispering."

I chuckled as I saw Bernie's side heave in what passed for his version of a kitty laugh. We sniped at each other occasionally, but since we'd been able to communicate with one another, I felt closer to him than I ever had. He was mouthy, snarky, and still the most loving cat I'd ever known, and I wouldn't trade him for anything, no matter what he really was.

"Where are we going next, my liege?" I asked as we popped out of the woods and ended up behind the cabin again.

"Back to Maddison House. I've got questions and I want some answers. I think that's the only place we're going to find them."

"Hey, I've got questions too. Lots of them. And no one ever seems to want to answer those."

The look Bernie shot me was fond as I opened the door to my car and let him in.

"Soon, Brynn. When things calm down, we'll have a pleasant talk, okay? For now, let's focus on dealing with this problem. I just hope Ned's wrong."

I pumped my fist in the air before sliding behind the wheel. That was the closest I'd ever gotten to him, promising to talk about his origins. I knew I'd eventually wear him down.

"I'm going to hold you to that, you know?"

Bernie shook his head as he looked out the window.

"I wouldn't expect anything less. Oh, and I'm hungry. The little morsel I had for lunch wasn't enough to feed a tiny bird."

I rolled my eyes and drove back down the mountain. We had more than enough time to head home before going back to the museum. By then, they should be closed, and I'd have a lot more opportunity to talk with the resident ghosts. Or so I hoped, anyway.

7

*B*y the time we made it back to Deadwood, the sun was setting behind the hills, and a definite chill was in the air. I held my arms against my chest as I stood outside the door of the Maddison House and wished I'd brought a coat.

"Are you too cold, buddy? I can leave the car running with the heater on if you want to stay out here."

"Not a chance. Let's get inside. It's got to be warmer in there."

I picked him up, punched in the code for the door, and slipped inside, latching the door behind me. Even though this was a small town, the last thing I needed was for some of the priceless antiques to go missing while I was talking to the resident ghosts. At least I hoped I'd be able to talk to them. I flipped on the lights and looked around the open area, trying to envision what it would have been like when it was used as a house instead of a historical museum.

Bernie squiggled out of my arms and thumped down on the floor, immediately heading for the stairs.

"Alright then, I guess I'll just check around down here."

I cautiously stepped forward, hoping I wouldn't have a repeat of yesterday's freezing, and headed over to the fireplace. The logs looked fake, so I hunted around for the ignition button. I didn't plan on being here long, but I wasn't averse to warming up my hands before searching for the elusive residents. I hit the button and held my hands up to the flames.

"I wish it had been that easy to get a fire going in my day," Bessie said, her voice echoing behind me.

"I can only imagine," I said, turning to face her with a welcoming smile. "It's good to see you."

I had a million questions for Bessie racing through my head, but I didn't want to scare her off. I turned back to the fire and continued warming my hands, watching out of the corner of my eye as she floated closer.

"Is that beastie of yours with you?"

"He is. He went upstairs. I promise he won't disturb anything."

I probably shouldn't have said that, but I wanted to put her at ease. I was pretty sure the worst thing he would do was shed over some furniture, but you never knew what could happen. Especially given what was going on here.

Bessie sniffed and edged closer.

"We'll see about that. Have you figured out our problem yet?"

"Not exactly, but I'm still researching it. Are any of the other residents around?"

"They'll be here soon. We like to have a nightcap and a chat before we retire for the evening."

I cocked my head to the side, amazed. Ghosts weren't able to enjoy drinking or eating, and rarely stuck to routines like humans did.

"That's incredible," I said before thinking. "You're so organized. Most spirits wander."

"I told you I run a tight ship. Things are a little different here than what you're used to, missy. I can tell you that. We like routine and we like nothing disrupting it. We may not know why we're still here, but while we are, we're going to do our jobs and stay civilized."

"They're coming."

I jumped in place as Bernie appeared at my feet, startling me.

"You always do that! Who's coming?"

Bessie narrowed her eyes at my cat and drifted towards the coffee table where an antique tea set was laid out.

"The other, um, residents, I guess you could say. Don't waste time. We need to get as much information as we can while they're all here. This place is strange."

"You can say that again," I said out of the corner of my mouth, glancing at Bessie in the hopes she hadn't heard us.

The chill in the room deepened, even with the fireplace going full blast. I edged closer to it as the light flickered gently. The forms of four people slowly came into view and I bit back a gasp as they all turned to look at me as one.

"Is this the girl?"

The woman spoke in a clipped British accent while raising an imperious eyebrow. She was dressed in what would have been the height of sophistication during the Victorian era. Her corset was laced so tightly her waist looked impossibly narrow, and for a second I realized how absurd it was that our generation brought back waist trainers.

Bessie nodded and floated closer.

"It is, mum. She's supposed to help us, but I'm not sure she's up to the task."

"Now, Bessie, that's no way to speak to a guest," said the man with the impressive handlebar mustache. "Our apologies, madam. I am William Thomas Maddison. This enchanting lady next to me is Lady Victoria Albright."

The British lady inclined her head ever so gracefully in my direction, but her eyes remained cold.

"Nice to meet you. I'm Brynn Sullivan."

"Of the Lancaster Sullivans?"

I turned to look at the other man and shook my head. His starched collar looked extremely uncomfortable, and I couldn't imagine spending my afterlife with my chin propped up that high.

"Not to my knowledge. And you are?"

He bowed deeply before straightening and clicking his heels together.

51

"Colonel Clarence Joseph of the 4th, the Queen's Own Hussars."

"Nice to meet you," I said, turning to the remaining ghost. "And what's your name?"

Compared to the other ghosts, she appeared to be the most shy. She was young, and her hair was still down around her shoulders, instead of piled on the top of her head like the other ladies.

"Arabella Stanhope."

Her voice was so quiet she was almost inaudible.

"It's nice to meet you all. Bessie was saying you gather like this nightly?"

Colonel Joseph nodded his head sharply and puffed out his chest.

"Routine is the glue that holds everything together," he said, pulling on the watch chain attached to his vest and peering at it. "We're actually two minutes late. We must do better."

I cocked my head, wondering how on earth his watch worked. Lady Victoria rolled her eyes as she swept closer to me, eyeing my jeans.

"I realize that today's fashions are much different. After all, I see guests wearing those daily, but don't you feel uncomfortable showing your nether regions to all and sundry?"

I choked a little and tried to smile.

"Lady Victoria, rein in that acid tongue of yours. It's obvious the girl is here to assist in our current difficulties," William said, his mustache bristling. "Forgive her, my dear girl. Now, how are you going to get rid of that thing that has been making our lives a living hell?"

"More like a dying hell," Lady Victoria said under her breath as she swept back towards the sofa and gracefully arranged herself. Bessie floated closer to her and took up her position behind the sofa.

It looked like the ghost of William Maddison was gritting his teeth as he lobbed an unfriendly glance in her direction. Bernie watched the byplay with a fascinated gleam in his eyes.

"You're the original owner of the house?" I asked, desperate to get this conversation back on track.

I wasn't sure how long they'd be able to manifest themselves, and

I didn't want to risk having to wait until tomorrow to ask more questions.

"That is correct. I built it myself."

He preened but seemed oblivious to the Colonel rolling his eyes. This was definitely an interesting group.

"He means he paid laborers to do it for him," the colonel said. "Now, as I asked before, what are you planning to do about our situation? We can't go on like this."

He rapped a heel on the floor and seemed disappointed when it made no sound.

"I'm still trying to figure out exactly what is happening. Can you describe when it started and anything odd you've noticed?"

The two men and Lady Victoria all started talking at once. I noticed Arabella shied away, her eyes frightened, as they got louder. I held up a hand and tried to restore order, but Bessie beat me to it.

"That's enough. I guess I have to do everything around here. Like I told you before, when you let that beast of yours on that clean bed, we don't have a complete concept of time as we'd like, despite this one's instance of running everything like it's a timed event. We simply know that one day everything was fine, and the next, we're being hounded by the very gates of hell. It's absolutely untenable. I've spent decades serving this house, and I simply cannot go on."

"When you say gates of hell, what do you mean?" Bernie said, his voice bringing instant silence to the room.

"Did that cat just talk?" Lady Victoria asked, her eyes widened to comical proportions.

"He does that," I said.

"Interesting. What Bessie means is that we have our routine here. Guests show up and we make the sounds and movements as necessary. Some people feel us, some don't. Some of us are more talented than others at making our manifestations known," she said, sparing a wry glance at the Colonel. "Everything was going swimmingly until it wasn't. Suddenly, things were flying back and forth, and when we tried to manifest, something dark and gruesome would appear, tossing us back into oblivion. This is the first time we've been able to meet at the same time in I don't know how long."

"When you say tossing back into oblivion, do you mean the ether?" I asked, watching their faces.

"The gray place," Arabella said.

"Yes, that's right," the Colonel said. "It bally well takes forever to re-form after that."

"Has it always been the five of you?"

The ghosts looked among themselves for a beat and I swore Arabella was going to say something, but snapped her mouth shut as Lady Victoria charged ahead.

"Of course. What an odd question."

I glanced down at Bernie, and he shook his head slightly.

"May I ask how you are all tied here? Mr. Maddison, I can see, since this was his house. How about the rest of you?"

"I worked my whole life here, and somehow I got lucky enough to spend my eternity here. If that preacher was still around, I'd give him a piece of my mind," Bessie said, shaking a finger. "Eternal life on a cloud, my foot. If I'd have known I'd get stuck here forever, I would have lived my life differently."

"Now, Bessie, don't say that. You were always my right hand when I was alive. I appreciate all of you've done," William said, floating closer to his former housekeeper.

I looked at the Colonel expectantly, and he shrugged his wide shoulders.

"I always had a bad ticker," he said, tapping his chest for emphasis. "It gave out when I was staying here and when I came to, here I was."

"And you, Lady Victoria?"

"I don't have the slightest idea, nor do I care to find out. I made the best of things in life and I intend to keep doing that in death."

"Arabella?"

The young girl shook her head, long curls flying. I noticed the other ghosts glance at each other and couldn't shake the feeling there was something more going on beneath the surface. I needed to talk to

54

her alone, without the other overbearing personalities sucking all the air out of the room.

"We can help you, you know," Bernie said, startling everyone again. "If anyone wants to move on, either right now or after this has been figured out, we can help."

Arabella's light gray eyes lit with a fierce hope, but it died quickly as she glanced around the room.

Lady Victoria contemplated me with narrowed eyes, tapping her elegant finger on her chin.

"We'll see. I can't speak for the others, of course, but I'm not in any hurry to join my husband. I just know he is waiting for me, and I have had more than enough of him in life."

I glanced between her and the Colonel, feeling slightly silly for imagining that they were together since they were both British. Lady Victoria followed my line of sight and snorted loudly.

"No, my dear. *That* is not my husband. May all the saints in heaven be praised."

The Colonel mumbled something, and I swore he flushed, something I didn't know ghosts could do.

"Well, the offer stands," I said, trying to break up the tension in the room. "But back to the thing that is bothering you and the guests here. Do any of you know what it could be?"

They all started talking at once, except for Arabella. She drifted towards the door and I noticed her form was wavering sharply. I was about to lose her.

"Ladies and gentleman," I said, holding up a hand. "One at a time."

"I think it's an evil spirit," Bessie said, nodding so hard her mobcap trembled again.

"I agree," Lady Victoria added. "It has to be a demon of some sort. What else could strike fear into our hearts?"

"Rancid ectoplasm," William Maddison said as he fingered his mustache. "That's the only explanation."

"Rancid what?"

"Never mind him, dear lady," the Colonel said, floating closer. "I believe it is a tormented soul who was drawn here for unfinished business."

"Arabella?"

I looked around the room, but she was gone. Dang it.

"She's been doing that lately, poor chuck," Bessie said. "I'll go to her."

"Yes, I believe it's time for me to retire as well," Lady Victoria said. "I trust you will handle everything to our satisfaction?"

I tried to look positive and capable as she leveled her eagle gaze at me, but I don't think I convinced her. She poofed out of sight, followed shortly by the Colonel and William.

I took a deep breath and looked at Bernie.

"What on earth do you make of that?"

"Other than the Colonel is the most sensible of the bunch? I don't know what to think. There are powerful undercurrents here."

"No kidding. Let's get out of here. Zane will be at my house soon."

I walked back to the fireplace and turned off the gas before walking to the door and flipping off the lights. I scooped Bernie into my arms and headed outside, bracing for the cold air.

"Who are you, and how did you get access to that building?"

I turned around and blinked as I looked at two handsome men standing on the sidewalk. For a second I thought I'd hit my head and was seeing double. They were tall, blond, and virtually identical, minus the way they parted their hair. I couldn't help but groan as I realized who they were. The wonder twins, er, ghost twins. Just what I needed. This day was definitely not going my way.

8

*B*ernie twisted in my arms, but I held my grip as I bit back a groan. Why did I have to run into these two right now? I glanced between the twins as I tried to come up with a reasonable reason for my being at the museum after hours that didn't involve mentioning ghosts or my abilities. A bright light flared behind them, and a camera crew came into view. This day couldn't get any better, could it?

"I'm sorry, I didn't catch your names?" I asked, stalling for time.

"We didn't offer them," said the twin on the left. "What are you doing here, and who are you?"

"My name's Brynn Sullivan. I'm an interior designer. The manager hired me to do a small project. What are you doing here, and who the heck are you?"

Twin number one, the one on the left, glanced over his shoulder at the camera with an incredulous expression. This was really feeling like a set-up.

"An interior designer? Shouldn't you be working during normal business hours?" asked the twin on the right.

"I don't believe that's any of your business. Do I need to call the sheriff? I have done nothing to either of you and you're both interrogating me. Who are you?"

At the mention of law enforcement, the twins tensed their shoulders at the same time and glanced at each other. Finally, twin number two, the one on the right, stepped closer and gave me what I'm sure he thought was an ingratiating smile. All he did was remind me of a hyena. A starving hyena.

"I'm so sorry, Brynn, was it? You just startled us. Are you aware of the issue with the hauntings at this location?"

"Well, it is billed as a haunted museum, so... yes?"

Twin number one, the one on the left, joined his brother and smiled so broadly I could see his back teeth. He clapped his brother on the arm as he looked at the camera and back at me.

"What Aiden means is we're professionals. I'm sure you've heard of us. We have a national television show, The Ghost Twins. We're professional ghost hunters. I'm Jaden, by the way."

He held out his hand, and I took it automatically, cringing as it felt like I was shaking hands with a dead fish.

"I'm sorry, but I don't know who you are. If you'll excuse me, I need to be on my way."

I side stepped, still holding onto Bernie tightly.

"Do you always take your cat with you? That seems, I dunno, kind of weird for an interior designer to do."

Aiden leaned closer, extending his finger towards Bernie's face. Even though I didn't like these two, the last thing I needed was for Bernie to bite them. He must have gotten the message and settled for hissing loudly. I could feel the growl building in his chest.

"I do. It's one of the many perks of being your own boss. I don't know what you want, but I'm leaving."

I started walking towards my car, and groaned aloud as the twins jogged after me, camera crew in tow.

"Are you a local? If you are, you should know there is a massive coverup being perpetrated on your town. Everyone from the museum manager to law enforcement is taking part."

I stopped and turned towards Jaden, not liking the smug grin he was wearing. The lights from the camera made me squint as I tried to focus on him.

"I don't know what you're talking about. But Russ and Dave are good people. I highly doubt they're covering anything up."

"Come on, bro, this is a waste of time. She's one of them. Heck, she's probably in on it. The manager will close the place down for quote unquote repairs, and they'll reopen as if there isn't any poltergeist in there. How many people are going to pay the price for their maliciousness?"

He pulled a sorrowful face as he looked at the camera and shook his head before pinning me with a glare.

Wow. I've experienced some intense and passionate people before, but these two took the cake. I looked at Aiden and shook my head.

"Why would you say something like that?"

"One of our viewers sent in a tip. And we're going to sort this out, even if it means we're risking our lives to do it."

Jaden moved his hand, catching my eye, and the camera lights cut off. I blinked as my eyes tried to adjust.

"That was fantastic, wasn't it? We can paste this scene in before we cut to a commercial," Aiden said.

"Totally, man. I really like how you amped up the energy there at the end. Epic."

I rolled my eyes and walked to my vehicle, completely over these two.

"Hey, we're not done with you yet."

"Yeah, I think you are," I said as I slid into the driver's seat.

I slammed the door and reversed out of my spot, thankful there was no one behind me. My hands were shaking a little as I turned around in the street and headed for home. I was never good with confrontation and being filmed in the process was possibly the most terrifying thing. And since I've dealt with banshees and other various creatures, that was saying something.

"It will be okay, Brynn," Bernie said, placing a paw on my arm.

"Are you kidding? That bit is going to be on national television and I looked like an idiot."

He shook his head, his eyes sparkling in the low light.

"You were professional and self-assured. They look like a bunch of blowhards."

"Well, it didn't feel like that at the moment. What do you think they're going to do?"

"I think they're going to make a big stink until they can gain access. They'll probably try to go around Russ and when they do, they'll set up their equipment and act official, even though they don't know what they're doing. Don't worry, Brynn. It will be okay."

I snorted and focused on the road, unconvinced. Growing up, my family had been aware of my abilities, and although my mom and dad supported me, they typically fell firmly into the camp of denial and hide. I couldn't imagine what they would think if they saw me on television like that.

I felt my stomach clench and took a few deep breaths. I knew there was nothing I could do to change it, and dwelling on it wasn't helping. I needed to change the subject.

"What do you think Zane is bringing for dinner?"

Bernie curled up on the seat and blinked at me.

"Fried chicken with all the fixings."

My stomach growled loudly, and I smiled.

"Well, I sure hope you're right."

"I always am."

A few minutes later, I pulled to a stop in front of my house and headed inside with Bernie. My stress melted away as I put Bernie's bag in its usual place by the door and went into the kitchen.

"Bernie, what can I fix you tonight?"

He wrapped his tail across my legs as he walked by.

"I'll take some of your chicken and maybe a few licks of your mashed potatoes."

I snorted a laugh as I grabbed a can of his food.

"You seem pretty confident about that. Just in case, I'll give you some chicken now."

"Sounds good to me. Don't you think it's a little odd that we could talk with the ghosts and didn't experience a recurrence of what happened the day before?"

I paused, my spoon in midair as I realized what he was saying. He had a point. We'd been in the Maddison House a much shorter time the day before, and had experienced the freezing terror twice. Tonight? Nothing. Huh. I went back to dishing up his food and slid the bowl in front of him.

"Maybe today is our lucky day, after all."

He rolled his eyes before digging into his food. I unloaded the dishwasher and pulled out a few plates for our supper as I waited for Zane. I was just checking my watch when I heard his Jeep outside.

"Don't forget to save me some chicken," Bernie said, talking with his mouth full.

"If we're having it, I will."

I opened the door for Zane, grinning as he swooped in to give me a kiss. I didn't miss the overnight bag he had slung over his shoulder and a warm zip worked its way down my spine.

"Hi, beautiful. Let me put these down so I can give you a proper hug."

I couldn't help but inhale as he walked past with the takeout bags. Dang it, the cat was right. Again.

"Told you," Bernie said, pausing as he washed up his face.

"Yeah, yeah."

Zane turned, quirking an eyebrow, and I rushed to explain.

"Bernie said you were picking up chicken. I didn't believe him, and now he's rubbing it in."

Zane laughed before pulling me into a hug. I rested my head on his hard chest, feeling the residual worry and stress fade away.

"Bernie's always right," he said, backing away so he could give me another lingering kiss. "I hope it was alright to bring a few things."

I nodded, feeling a flush spread across my cheeks as he put the bag in the hall.

Bernie hopped on the table and stuck his head in a bag, rustling around.

"Score, he brought corn. And Zane is completely correct."

I grabbed the plates and started dishing out the food as Zane scratched Bernie under his chin. Once everything was ready, we both dug in while Bernie waited patiently on the other side of the table.

"Tell me about your day," Zane asked, in between bites.

"It was interesting," I said, loading up my fork with mashed potatoes.

I relayed what the ghosts had to say while he listened with rapt attention, chicken temporarily forgotten.

"That's just amazing," he said, picking up his piece again. "The things they would have seen through the years. I wish I could talk to them."

"Tell him about the twins, Brynn."

Bernie's little face was serious and, although I didn't want to ruin the mood, Zane needed to know what happened.

"After that, Bernie and I ran into some television stars."

Zane cocked his head as I went through my encounter with the wonder twins. By the time I was finished, his light blue eyes had a steely glint to them.

"The next time you see them, and I'm sure there will be a next time, call me. I don't care what I'm doing. I'll be there in ten minutes. I don't want you to deal with them alone."

I waved off his concern and focused on my corn on the cob.

"I'm sure they were just trying to fill in their footage with some... what would they call it? Local color. I wouldn't worry about it."

Zane placed a warm hand over mine and locked eyes with me.

"I can tell you're upset and I don't like that. Seriously, Brynn. You're not alone anymore. I know you can take care of yourself, but I'm here if you need me."

My heart melted at his serious expression and I nodded, feeling a lump in my throat.

"I will. Hopefully I won't see them again, though."

We spent the rest of our meal catching up on his day, which had been pretty quiet. I told him about my trip to the library and lunch with Logan, and by the time we were done, we were both laughing and at ease. I gave Bernie his requested chicken, and, of course, a lick of my mashed potatoes, before going to the kitchen to clean up.

"That was amazing, but I ate way too much," Zane said as he helped me load the dishwasher.

"Me, too. What do you want to do now?"

Butterflies attempted to swarm in my stomach, although they had little room for flight after my meal, and I started wiping down the already clean counters to give my hands something to do. I wasn't in the habit of having overnight guests, even though he'd stayed over the night before. Zane looked at me before taking the rag and hanging it over the sink to dry.

"Let's watch a little television and go from there," he said, giving me a gentle smile.

He took my hand and led me to the couch, where we cuddled close. I flipped on the set and started browsing through the channels as Bernie joined us.

"What do you want to watch?"

The lights flickered as he answered. Bernie sat bolt upright, fur on end, and stared into the corner of the room.

"Brynn..." he said, before hissing loudly.

Zane looked at the cat before searching my face.

"What's going on? Why's he acting like that?"

I tried to answer, but stopped as a powerful wind swept through my living room, bringing with it a cold so severe I thought my bones would snap. We were frozen in place as terror clawed at my throat. I wanted to move, but all I could do was whimper as my mind tried to make sense of what was going on.

The television flickered, and my eyes were drawn to the screen, where a hideous face was briefly visible. I tried to scream, but my voice wouldn't work. The cabinets in the kitchen slammed open and shut as the lights went off and on rapidly. It was like being trapped in the world's worst rave.

Bernie puffed up to three times his size, green eyes blazing, and started chanting something I couldn't understand as he approached the corner of the room. Slowly, ever so slowly, my limbs unlocked and the feeling of cold faded. I turned my head towards Zane, alarmed by his expression.

He was a powerful man, resilient and easy going. Right now, he looked frozen in fear.

"Zane?"

His breath hitched, and he looked at me, eyes wild. Bernie rushed over and hopped on the couch, placing a paw on Zane's arm. Zane blinked and shuddered out a breath, followed by another one. He closed his eyes, and I scooted across the couch so I could put my arms around him. A shuddering sob shook his chest, and he squeezed his eyes shut.

"I'm so sorry, Brynn."

"Don't be," I said, brushing my fingers down his chiseled face. "Are you okay?"

He nodded and reached a hand out to stroke Bernie's soft fur. My cat crawled into his lap and cuddled close, purring loudly.

"I haven't been that afraid since I was back with my unit. When it happened..."

He stopped, and I pulled him close.

"It's okay. If you want to talk about it, I'm here. If you don't want to talk, that's okay, too."

Zane never talked about his time with the military, but I knew there was something under the surface.

"Not right now, if that's okay. Soon. I know we need to talk about it."

"Whenever you're ready, I'm here. Whatever I can do to help you, I will."

Bernie kneaded his paws on Zane's leg, letting him know that even though they couldn't talk, he was there for him, too. I looked at Bernie, making eye contact as we both comforted Zane. I guess we now knew why we had experienced nothing at the Maddison House. Somehow, whatever was there had followed us home.

"We're safe," Bernie whispered. "It will be okay. I won't let anything else happen tonight."

I trusted my cat as we all cuddled close, determined to shove the thoughts of terror to the back of my mind. Somehow, we were going to figure this out, but right now, I just wanted to hold everyone close and not think about it.

9

*W*hen my eyes opened the next morning, I felt as though someone was watching me. My heart beat stuttered before I realized the person watching me sleep was Zane. My cheeks flushed as I rolled over to look at him. The corners of his eyes were crinkled as he smiled at me, and my heart sped up for a different reason.

"Good morning, gorgeous," he said, tracing his finger down the side of my face.

I squinched up my eyes and stuck my tongue out at him.

"I think that's my line. I'm well aware of how I look first thing in the morning."

I felt around my hair to confirm that, yep, it was a tangled mess on my head. After what happened the night before, we'd fallen into bed shortly after everything calmed down and I didn't take the time to braid my hair.

"About last night," Zane said, looking away.

I rested my hand on his sculpted chest and interrupted him.

"I'm so sorry about that. Whatever we're dealing with, it must have followed us home. It's my fault."

He rolled onto his side and looked at me, eyes serious as they searched my face.

"It's not your fault. I'm, well, I'm embarrassed at how I reacted. You should be able to rely on me. I'm your rock, and last night, I crumbled. You deserve better than that."

My first instinct was to roll my eyes and make a joke about men and how they feel like they always have to be the strong ones, but something made me pause. He wasn't kidding. I searched for the perfect words before deciding to speak from the heart.

"Zane, you'll always be my rock. We're both human, though, and we both have different things to deal with. You've helped me deal with my past in more ways than you'll probably ever realize. I understand that you've been through things that were much worse. You haven't talked about it, but I feel it in my heart," I said, touching my chest. "I will never judge you, or think less of you, because you had a human reaction. Whenever you're ready to talk about what you experienced, I'm here for you. If you never want to talk about it, that's okay, too."

Zane stared up at the ceiling, his face conflicted. I knew it was different for men, especially with expressing their emotions, so I waited and traced a pattern on the comforter until he answered.

"Brynn, that means more to me than you'll ever know. I've never been this... vulnerable to anyone before. It's a new feeling. I'm not saying I don't want to talk about it, just that I'm not ready to talk about it right now. In fact, when I left the service, I thought I'd never have to deal with it again. I see now that was a dream. I just wanted to... thank you for being there, I guess."

He let out a sigh, clearly frustrated with trying to put his feelings into words. I winked at him before reaching for his middle and applying some well-placed tickles.

"When it happens, it happens. Now, let's go get some breakfast. Last one in the kitchen is a rotten egg."

The sound of his laughter warmed my heart as I vaulted out of bed and scampered down the hall. I found Bernie waiting in front of the counter with his food.

"Hey, bud, how long have you been up?"

"Long enough to know you two needed a little privacy for the talk that's been brewing inside of Zane since last night. You two okay?"

I nodded as I reached up and grabbed a can of his food.

"Thank you for that. We are."

"Good, then hurry with that food. I'm starving."

I snorted as I dished up his meal and started looking through the cabinets. Our French toast from the day before had cleaned me out of bread, and there weren't many options in the fridge either. I was standing in front of it when Zane appeared, his hair still wet from a shower.

"Hey, rotten egg," I said, holding my cheek up for a kiss. "I think I'll have to give you a raincheck on breakfast. I'm pretty close to being out of anything edible, unless you want to reheat some of that Chinese food you brought the other day."

I wrinkled my nose at the thought of spicy food this early in the morning, and Zane let out a chuckle that made his shoulders shake.

"I think I'll pass and, based on your expression, that's probably a good thing. I can grab something on my way to work."

"What do you have planned for today?"

"I've got to meet with that potential client in an hour. After that, I've got some office work I've been putting off that needs to be tackled."

"Sounds like fun."

"Then I'm telling it wrong. How about you?"

I poked him in the side before following him to the door. Bernie jogged behind us, licking his chops.

"Research. While you two were sleeping, I came up with a few ideas."

"Um, I guess research," I said, filling Zane in on my marching orders. "I'll text you if anything interesting comes up."

Zane leaned close, planting a kiss on my lips that quickly deepened into something more. I was left gasping as we came up for air, and he was wearing a wicked grin.

"I'll do the same. Be careful, okay, Brynn?"

I nodded and marveled at his ability to think about anything else besides that kiss.

"You, too. Did you want to do something later?"

His wicked grin came back and his eyes sparkled.

"I think we can come up with something. Stay out of trouble, Sullivan."

"Back at you, Matthews."

I closed the door after watching him get in his Jeep and leaned against it, heart fluttering. Bernie's sharp meow startled me, and my eyes flew open to see him staring at me.

"You two are something else."

My hand moved up to my lip and I couldn't help but smile, as it felt like I was walking on a cloud on my way back to the kitchen. He hopped up on the counter and looked at me, his little kitty face serious, and I quickly came back to earth.

"Thank you for protecting us last night. I don't know what we would've done without you."

He lashed his tail back and forth before getting settled.

"I'm always here for you. We have a problem, though. It took everything I had to repel that spirit and it's getting stronger. We need to find out who we are dealing with. Once we have a name, we'll gain some power over it, but that might not be enough."

His warning sobered me. Bernie tended towards the dramatic, but I knew he wasn't playing around. I nodded and put my hands on my hips.

"Do we need to go back to the library? I haven't even looked at the book Sophie gave me."

"I think we can do the bulk of our research from here. We need to look into the current residents of the Maddison House. I know we were distracted with the twin power tools, but we need to get back on track. The ghosts were hiding something and we need to figure out what that is."

A laugh burbled in my chest at his description of the Ghost Twins.

"I'm totally stealing that nickname. I love it."

Bernie gave his equivalent of a kitty eye roll.

"Focus, Brynn. We have little time."

Disturbed, I grabbed my bag with my laptop and set up shop at my kitchen table. His warning had the unintended consequence of completely killing my appetite, and I didn't even bother getting ready for the day. Obviously, whatever we needed to find was important.

"Okay, bud. I guess we'll go through and see what we can find on each ghost. You remember their names, right?"

He hopped on the table and sat next to my laptop, glancing over his shoulder at me.

"Of course. Don't you?"

I mumbled something about know-it-all cats that made his whiskers quirk and booted up my computer.

"Alright, let's start with Colonel Mustard."

"Don't you mean Joseph?"

"You can't steal all my fun. What regiment was he with?"

"The 4th, the Queen's Own Hussars."

"What's a Hussar?"

"The term originated in Hungary, and referred to the members of the cavalry. The British first raised their Hussars in the 1600s, and then..."

"Got it, cavalry," I said, ignoring Bernie's huff.

My cat was a bit of a history buff, and by that I mean a total nut. If I'd let him, I would have heard the origins of the entire British military before he was done and although I'm sure it would've been interesting, I wanted to focus on the task at hand.

"What are you finding?"

I glanced at my cat, who was reading the screen faster than I could.

"I literally just typed in his name. The odds of finding anything are pretty small."

"What's that?" Bernie asked, gesturing with a paw towards my screen.

I clicked on the link and let out a whistle as I read through an old archive of The London Times.

"It appears our Colonel was a highly decorated soldier. Huh, it says here he was in ranks with Winston Churchill. Would you look at that?"

"They didn't actively serve in India, did they?"

I looked at Bernie, distracted.

"Why?"

"Just curious. I'm trying to narrow down what we're dealing with."

"And it could be something from India that followed the Colonel, here? Is that what you're getting at?"

"Maybe. Keep reading."

I shook my head as I settled back into the archives and kept searching. After a few minutes, it was obvious I would find nothing else.

"I don't think so, bud. From the timeline, he may have served during a peaceful period. I'm guessing he came over here before the first World War."

"Hmm, there goes that theory. Onto the next one."

We spent the next two hours going through each ghost's name, and coming up empty. While they were all interesting people in their own right, nothing seemed to show that any of them would have a powerful entity out for revenge. Bessie came up nearly empty, except for a brief mention in the article dealing with William Maddison's death, and Lady Victoria was very hard to pin down. Our last shot was Arabella Stanhope, and I wasn't full of hope.

I dutifully typed her name into my search engine and went into the kitchen to brew some coffee. I wasn't used to functioning this much without it, and frankly, I was surprised I was doing so well. I waited for the coffee to drip before heading back to my laptop, where Bernie was currently entranced.

"Anything, Bern?"

"I'm not sure... but I think we're on to something here," he said, staring at the screen. "See what you think."

I quickly forgot my coffee as I read the tragic story of Arabella. She'd been found dead in the house's yard in the 1918. She wasn't a local girl, and no one knew who she was, or how she ended up there.

The only reason she'd been identified was a letter she'd been carrying in her purse when she was found.

I sat back in my seat, overwhelmed. That poor girl.

"What do we do now, Bernie?"

He heaved a sigh and thumped down to the floor.

"We need to talk to her, but I have a feeling that will not be easy. You saw how she was last night."

"We'll do that tonight. What should we do in the meantime?"

"Me? I'm going to take a much needed nap. What you do until tonight is completely up to you."

I shook my head as he stalked back to my bedroom. I guess that told me. I poured myself a cup of coffee and tried to come up with a plan. I glanced at the bag on my kitchen table and spotted the book Sophie gave me. Well, if nothing else, I could research different malevolent entities and see if I could figure out what was coming after us. That sounded like a blast. I polished off my cup and poured another one before grabbing the book and heading for the couch. I might as well get comfortable.

10

*T*he hour I spent reading through the book was enough to leave me doubting whether I'd ever sleep soundly again. Even though I felt like I was fairly familiar with the paranormal world, this book shook me to my core. There was obviously a lot out there I didn't understand, and to be honest, I wasn't ready.

Bernie was still in bed and I was feeling restless as I paced around the house. On my third lap, past my bedroom door, my cat raised his dark head from my pillow and glared at me.

"Can't you find something productive to do? Or are you going to continue waking me up?"

"Oh, you're up," I said, breezily ignoring his irritation. "Do you want to do anything?"

"Yes. I want to sleep. Holding back whatever that thing was took everything out of me."

I instantly felt like a monster.

"Sorry, bud. I'll find something to do. I need to pick up a few design clients, so I'm not in your hair so much."

His fierce gaze softened and he let out a little chirp that made me smile.

"You're never in my hair. But I am tired. Why don't you go to the police office and see if you can search through their arrest records? It was useful a few months ago. It might prove useful again."

"Great idea! Why didn't I think of that?"

Bernie muttered something that sounded like he was doing the thinking for both of us, but I blew him a kiss as I grabbed a fresh pair of jeans and a hoodie.

"I sure hope I can find what we need. The last time we were there, you were the one who found the records we needed on Molly."

"I have a feeling you'll be fine. Good night."

Molly McElhone was a ghost who'd been so tormented in life and in death that she'd turned into a banshee. I paused as I tugged the hoodie over my head. Maybe that was similar to what was going on here. And then again, Molly hadn't slammed doors. So, maybe not. I kissed Bernie on the top of his furry little head before heading out.

The drive to the sheriff's office in Deadwood was pleasant, and I admired the changing leaves on the hillsides. Since Zane was new to the area, I made a note to take him on a drive through a nearby scenic canyon where the fall foliage was always spectacular. Now that the leaves were changing, it wouldn't be long before the entire area was covered with a thick blanket of snow.

I texted Zane as I walked into the building, and stopped at the duty desk, where the usual deputy was trying to look engaged, but failing miserably.

"Hey, Donald. Is the sheriff in?"

"He is Miss Brynn. Go on back."

I waved at him as I walked down the hall and found Dave, feet propped on his desk as usual, with his cowboy hat pushed back on his head.

"Hi, Dave. Looks like you're busy as usual," I said, plopping into the seat across from his desk.

"I'll have you know I've been run ragged lately. Those dang tv twins are sorely trying my patience."

I grimaced as I remembered my encounter with the not so dynamic duo.

"I hear you. I met them last night. They're... something."

"That's putting it nicely. What do you need today?"

I smiled as I thought back to how scared I'd been of Dave when I was a teenager. I sat in the same chair and tried to convince him to help me with a cold case. Since then, he'd become accepting of what I could do, and I no longer needed to do complicated mental gymnastics to convince him to help.

"Remember how I said I'd been hired by the manager at the Maddison House? Well, I'm looking into some strange things and found that one ghost was a murder victim back in the early 1900s. I was hoping you wouldn't mind if I went through the records?"

"Not at all. Since the last time you were here, I had Pete do a clean sweep of that room. I think you'll find it a lot easier to get what you're looking for. Why don't you tell me about it while we walk back there?"

He swung his long legs off the desk and motioned for me to go ahead of him through the door. I told him what I'd learned so far, but kept the creepy element out of it. Dave was a believer, but there was no need for him to know everything.

"So, I'm thinking the, um, entity, might have something to do with the murderer of the girl," I said, finishing up my story. "So, I'm hoping there's a record of the case and I'll find a little more information."

He swung open the door to the archive and I couldn't help but gasp as I walked in. The dusty room had been completely transformed. All the file boxes were stacked neatly, and a quick glance at the labels on the shelves told me everything was now organized by date. Bernie was right. I didn't need his help to find what I was looking for. This time, at least.

"Wow. Pete did an amazing job," I said, walking around the room. "It must have taken him ages."

"I had him work on it after that murder up at the cabin. He needed a little time away from the field and this fit the bill nicely."

Dave had to be one of the nicest people in law enforcement I'd ever met. Pete was a younger deputy, and that case had been gruesome. That he'd cared enough about Pete to do that spoke volumes about his character.

"Well, the next time I see him, I'll have to thank him."

"Do you want any help?"

"If you have nothing else going on, that would be great," I said, eying the stack of boxes. "We're looking for an unsolved murder back in 1918."

He walked down the row and grabbed two boxes down from the top shelf. If nothing else, given how short I was, it was a good thing he was there to help.

"I'll take one, and you can go through the other," he said, pushing one box towards me. "Do we have a month in mind? Pete stacked the boxes according to their dates, but he didn't organize the contents."

"September," I said as I opened the top of my box. "There wasn't an exact date of her death in the article, but that should narrow it down."

I started paging through the arrest reports, doing my best not to get distracted by the petty crimes that occurred back in the town's founding history. Some of them were quite amusing, while a few, like Arabella's death, were heartbreaking. I stayed focused and made it halfway through the box when Dave's sharp laugh distracted me.

"What?"

"Sorry, just reading about a report on a barking dog," he said, glancing over at me. "The person reporting it is related to a lady here in town who is a frequent caller. I guess some things never change."

Dave wasn't kidding when he said the contents of the boxes weren't organized. I stacked reports by month, figuring that if I ever had to go through these again, it would be nice to have them ordered.

"Here, I think I found something. You said her name was Arabella, right?"

"Yes, Arabella Stanhope. It's such a pretty name."

He put the report on the table and we both bent over it, skimming it quickly.

"It says here that there were two persons of interest in the case, but neither one could be found. Thomas Morrow and Stanley Grisholm."

"Huh. I guess people who name their kids strange names aren't a new thing."

"Stanley? That's a pretty common name, even today."

"No, Thomas Morrow. Get it? Tom Morrow. Tomorrow?"

Dave rolled his eyes, and we went back to reading.

"She was found the morning of September 8th, so the murder either took place the night of the 7th or early that morning."

"That's interesting," I said, pulling my phone out to confirm today's date. "The anniversary of her death is tomorrow or the next day. I wonder if that explains what's going on? Is there anything else on her?"

"I doubt it. It looks to me like they didn't try very hard to track down either man. Let's double check, though."

We were both quiet as we continued searching through the records. My heart hurt at the thought of a sweet girl like Arabella being killed and no one bothering to investigate it properly. She deserved justice.

I hit the bottom of my box and sighed. Nothing. Dave shook his head as he finished looking through his.

"That's it. I don't know if it's worth going through the following year to see if there was a follow-up. I'm guessing they figured she was just passing through. The report says she had no known next of kin."

I stacked the papers back into the box and shut the lid.

"Well, at least we have two names to go on. That's more than I had when I walked in here. Thanks for going through these with me."

"I know it's likely everyone involved at the time is long gone, but if there's anything I can do to help solve this one, let me know. I can try to track down any relatives she might have had. I'll make a copy of this report for you."

"Thanks, Dave," I said, putting a hand on his arm. "I appreciate you caring."

"More should have been done back then. I can't change it, but if I can help now, I will," he said, his tone gruff. "What will you do now?"

"I think I'll head back to the library and see if I can search for these two names through the old newspaper archives. Maybe we'll get lucky. I might need to come back and go through more files. Is that okay?"

"Always, Brynn. Make yourself at home. I'll let Donald know to let you through, just in case I'm not here."

I followed him back to his office and waited while he made me a copy of the incident report. We'd come a long way in the past year and it felt good to have Dave in my corner. He handed me the sheet and tipped his hat.

"Let me know what you find."

"Will do. Thanks again for this."

I left the station and headed straight for the library. While I'd hoped for more information, at least I had a crumb to follow. Maybe it would lead to more. My phone dinged with a text from Zane as I walked into the library, and I paused by the doors to answer him and let him know my next steps. After last night, I was determined to figure out what was going on. I wasn't sure Zane could take a recurrence of what happened. To be honest, I wasn't sure I wanted to experience anything like it again, either. I walked inside, ready to see what I could uncover.

11

*S*tacia was at the front desk, bent over her computer, as I walked into the library. She glanced up and gave me a warm smile.

"Sophie was right. She had a feeling you'd been in today," she said, rummaging under the counter. "She asked me to make sure you got this. If you didn't show up, she was planning on calling you."

She held out a flowered envelope across the desk and I couldn't help but chuckle when I saw Sophie's characteristic swirly hand-writing on it.

"Is she in today?"

"She just left for a doctor's appointment, but she'll be in later if you want to come back."

My heart twinged, and I gripped the envelope a little tighter. Sophie wasn't getting any younger. She'd been such a fixture in my life I couldn't help but worry about her.

"I hope it isn't serious."

Stacia waved her hand and shook her head.

"She said it was a routine check-up. I'm sure it's nothing to worry about. Did you need anything?"

I let out the breath I was holding and relaxed.

"I want to check out some archives for the paper. If you need to man the desk, it's fine. I know where everything is."

Stacia looked relieved as she ran a hand through her hair.

"If you don't mind, that would be great. I'm still learning the ropes here and I'd hate to get in trouble if I'm not up front when someone comes in."

"No worries. I'll put everything back."

I headed towards the Dakota Room and looked down at the envelope. Once I claimed a table and unloaded my bag, I gently lifted the flap of the envelope. Sophie loved stationary, and the last thing I wanted to do was rip through the delicate paper. Her large scrawl dominated the sheet.

Brynn - I found something this morning that I thought might interest you. In fact, you may already know, so forgive me if you do. I believe the spirit you're dealing with may be a wraith. They are associated with powerful emotions, such as rage and fear. They are associated with the recently deceased, and feed off of souls, living and dead, to sustain themselves. From what I could find, it seems they differ from other spirits. Be careful, my dear. I'll be in touch soon. Until then, I hope your day is filled with whimsy, wonder, and... I'll let you fill in the blank.

"And wackiness," I said out loud, reeling from the information. "I guess it's better than wraiths."

I shook off that disconcerting thought and focused on my first order of business. I needed to learn more about Thomas Morrow and Stanley Grisholm. I logged into the library computer and went to the special app they'd created for the local newspapers. While the project was a work in progress, the library had almost finished digitizing the papers back to when they first started during the gold rush.

I typed in the first name and waited for the results, only to be disappointed. Nothing came up for Thomas Morrow. I frowned and typed in Stanley's name. This time, I was rewarded with a few hits. I paged through each one, learning that Mr. Grisholm was the town vagrant back in the day, and had been arrested many times for drunkenness in public, loitering, and a host of other petty crimes. He'd died of exposure in the 1920s. If Sophie was right, and we were dealing with a wraith, he wasn't the man, er, spirit, we were looking for. I sat back and tapped my fingers on the desk.

There was nothing to show he had any violent tendencies. If I had to guess, I think he was the common scapegoat back then, but the police didn't have any reason to believe he'd killed a young girl. That meant I needed to dig deeper on Thomas Morrow.

I closed the app and opened the browser. Since I had found nothing in the local papers, that could have meant he'd moved away from the area. I typed in his name and almost cheered when I got a hit from a paper in Wyoming. It was a recent obituary. Bingo!

My eyes widened as I read through the article. He'd apparently lived to the ripe old age of one-hundred-and-twenty. What? How was that possible? The article listed his death as occurring earlier this year. I grabbed a piece of paper and wrote his birth year of 1902 and did the math. If he was the killer, he would have been just sixteen when he committed the crime. That didn't seem plausible, but everything was making sense.

I glanced back at Sophie's letter and blinked. If he was a wraith, that made sense of how he could live for so long. I went back to the obituary and kept reading.

By the time I finished the piece, I'd learned that Thomas was definitely in South Dakota at the right time period, and moved to Wyoming shortly after 1918. Everything made sense, but I wasn't sure what to do with this information. I needed to talk to Bernie.

I packed my things back up and shut down the computer as my mind raced with possibilities. It seemed fantastical, but somehow, it was the only thing that made sense.

I walked back to the front of the library and thanked Stacia before heading back outside to my car. By the time I got home, I had so many questions I didn't even know where to start. I burst inside and walked back to my room, where Bernie was still cuddled into my pillow.

"Bernie, do you know what wraiths are?"

He practically levitated, fur sticking in a dozen different directions, and leveled his emerald glare in my direction.

"Don't you knock?"

"Hey, you always wake me up."

He sat on the bed and began licking his fur into place, stopping every few seconds to mutter and glare.

"I never flounce in and announce we're dealing with perhaps the most terrifying spiritual entity that exists. I can guarantee that."

"Okay, fine. I apologize. Now that you're awake, are we dealing with a wraith?"

He stopped grooming and looked at me, his little face serious.

"You know, it's entirely possible. What makes you think that?"

I sat on the bed, opening my arms so he could crawl on my lap, and told him about Sophie's letter and what I'd learned. I needed the comfort of his fuzzy body, and I think he needed the cuddle, too. I couldn't help but ask but what on my mind once I'd finished my story.

"How is it possible he lived to be that old? I mean, I guess it happens from time to time, but that seems odd."

"If he is a wraith, it explains everything. It also means that Ned was right," Bernie said, hopping down from the bed. "I've never dealt with one, but I've heard stories. All I can say is we're going to need all the help we can get."

And with that, he stalked out of the room, shouting about how hungry he was, and it was so hard to get food around here. I rolled my eyes before trailing after him, and dishing up his food in the kitchen.

"What should our next move be? I mean, I guess I need to learn more about wraiths so we know what we're dealing with. I can read while you're eating."

"After that, I suggest another trip to Maddison House. I know it's earlier in the day than we'd like, but we can't afford to waste time. If you are correct, the longer we wait, the worse it will be."

I swallowed hard before putting his bowl in front of him and heading to the living room to grab the book I'd been reading earlier. I paged through it until I found the section on wraiths. I'd glanced at it before, but to be honest, it seemed so far out, I'd had a hard time believing it. I read the section with a fresh outlook and by the time I was done, I'd learned more than I cared to.

Bernie joined me on the couch and placed a paw on the book.

"How much of this do you think is accurate?" I asked.

"Most of it. Some of these accounts are tainted by hearsay, but I think you can see the big picture."

"So, these wraiths artificially prolong their lives by consuming the souls of things both living and dead, correct?"

Bernie nodded before swiping his muzzle with a paw. When he did things like that, it comforted me somehow. I knew he was more than a cat, but seeing him do catlike things absurdly put my mind at ease.

"That's right. Some wraiths have lived for hundreds of years doing that. Eventually, though, they need more to sustain them and it becomes harder to fill that need. They end up burning out and finally dying."

"What happens to their soul? Can they pass on? What happens to the souls that get consumed?"

"Honestly?" Bernie said, making eye contact briefly. "I don't know. You've seen the other side, the good side, and you know it's there. There's another side, the one you haven't seen. I would guess that all creatures have their place in the afterlife. The ether you've experienced is a, well, it's a holding ground of sorts. I think when this wraith appears, it takes a little of the ether with it. As for the souls consumed, I wish I knew. I only know that there is justice in this world and the next."

"Okay," I said, drawing out the word. "What I don't understand is let's say he was a wraith while he was alive? Why is he still active now that's he gone? Wouldn't he have gone to one of the two places? I'm guessing since he was a wraith, he wouldn't have gone to the good place."

"I'm not sure," he said, kneading the couch fabric with his claws. "I've dealt with nothing like this before. I would assume if he had enough rage fueling him, he might run from where he's supposed to be to escape judgment."

"Is there like an afterlife warden who should chase him down? Can we file a report or something?"

I knew I wasn't making sense, but none of this made sense in any slightest interpretation of the word. Bernie huffed out a laugh and shook his head.

"If there was, we wouldn't need people like you in the world, Brynn. You help ghosts pass over to their reward. I guess you're the warden."

"So this falls to me?"

The thought filled me with dread. In my few interactions with the being that was Thomas Morrow, if it was indeed him, I'd been overwhelmed and woefully unprepared. Knowing that he was a wraith was great and all, but that didn't mean I knew what I was doing.

"It does," Bernie said, giving me a nod. "And you may not realize it, but you're more than capable. I trust that when the time is right, you'll know what needs to be done. I'll be here every step of the way, supporting you."

I ruffled the fur on the top of his head and tried to smile. His faith in me was great, but I could only hope it would be enough.

"All right, bud. Well, let's head to the museum. Maybe we can find some answers there."

I drove back to Deadwood in silence, trying to make sense of the thoughts running through my head. Bernie looked out the window and was uncharacteristically quiet as I drove. I pulled into a parking space and looked at the Maddison House, imagining what it would have been like back when it was built. A lot had changed since then, but from the age of the neighboring buildings, I assumed they'd all been built at the same time. How had Thomas Morrow killed Arabella and tossed her in the yard? I shook off the thought and gathered Bernie in my arms before sliding out of my seat.

There weren't many cars parked nearby, and I perked up as I walked inside. Maybe I'd be able to contact the ghosts since the place wasn't overrun with tourists. Norma was standing in the lobby as I entered, and the smile she gave me was pleasant, if a little confused.

"Oh, hello again," she said, going back to her dusting. "I thought you were coming at night. I'm surprised to see you here."

I wasn't sure how she knew that, but figured Russ must have said something. She didn't seem to notice Bernie in my arms, and I wasn't about to bring it up. I went with it. Seems like I've been doing a lot of that these days.

"I came last night, but I wanted to check on a few things during the day," I said, remembering my cover story of doing some interior design work. "Do you mind if I go upstairs?"

"Go right ahead. We're usually much busier than this, but hopefully next month it will pick up."

As I walked up the stairs, I realized next month was October, which meant Deadwood would go all out with their holiday celebrations. A haunted museum was the perfect attraction for Halloween. If I couldn't get this wraith thing figured out by then... my thought trailed off, forgotten, as Bessie popped into view at the top of the stairs.

She motioned for me to follow her into a bedroom. I looked at Bernie and he gave a kitty shrug before squirming out of my arms and following her. I was right on his heels, and nearly tripped over him, when he halted.

Bessie's face was drawn and her eyes were darting from side to side. Given her usual stoic nature, I could sense something was very wrong.

"Bessie, are you okay?"

Her mobcap trembled as she shook her head.

"No, ma'am. I am not. I seriously doubt if anything is going to be okay."

I blinked, surprised at her tone. She seemed like the last person, well, ghost, to be dramatic about anything. Except maybe cat hair on a bed.

"What's wrong?"

"The black thing came back. But this time it was worse. Much worse. It's William. He's gone."

"Gone? Does he not have enough energy to manifest?" I asked, cocking my head to the side.

"It's not that. We were all together this morning when that thing came back. It came for Arabella this time, and he darted in front of it. Just like that, he was gone. We've been calling and calling, but I can no longer sense him. It's just like..."

She cut off and looked away. Bernie walked towards her and fastened his eyes on her. She stared at him, seemingly unable to look away.

"It's just like what? The sixth ghost who you've yet to mention?"

Her shoulder slumped and her mobcap trembled again.

"Yes. Peter. He was the first to disappear. We've waited, hoping he would return, but it's been weeks. I fear he's gone."

I held up my hand, confused.

"So, there was another ghost here, and he disappeared?"

"Yes. I'm sorry we didn't tell you before. It's like it's hunting us, one by one. Lady Victoria is bereft. She's certain she's next. It's all I can do to keep everyone together."

I could tell the admission hurt, but she squared her formidable shoulder and finally met my gaze.

"Please help us."

"I'll do what I can. I think I know what we're dealing with, but a few pieces of the puzzle are missing. I need to speak with Arabella."

"After the scare this morning, I doubt she'll come back for a day or two. It took her a week after Peter left."

Frustration made me grit my teeth. I knew Arabella was shy, and getting her to talk about her murder wouldn't be easy, but I'd hoped to try.

"Has she said anything about her passing?" I asked.

Bessie's eyes narrowed, and she stared at me before nodding slowly.

"Once. Only once. The rest of them go on about it, remembering, but she doesn't like to speak of it. She said she'd received a letter from a boy, asking her to meet on the steps of the house. That's all she remembers, though, before waking in the garden. As soon as I spotted her, I took her under my wing. She's a delicate thing. It's taken her eons to interact with us. I don't know, but I'm guessing that boy was the one who killed her."

I nodded while I chewed on my lip. It made sense. Somehow, the two must have known each other. The letter identified her, and if it had been signed by Thomas Morrow, it made sense that's why the cops were looking at him at the time of her death. I wished I had more information.

"Bessie, I..." My words were cut off by loud voices downstairs. I looked at Bernie before walking out of the room to the top of the stairs.

"We absolutely can be here," a familiar voice said. "The board has granted us all-access. We need to get our equipment set-up imme-diately."

I groaned and rubbed at my eyes. This was the last thing I needed.

12

*M*y feet were poised to carry me down the stairs, but my phone buzzed with a call from Zane. I glanced at Bernie and he nodded sharply before going down the stairs.

"Have him come. I have a feeling we might need him."

I accepted the call and smiled as Zane's warmth came through the line.

"How's my favorite girl?"

"Hey, I thought I was your only girl," I said. "Things are... interesting right now."

"Of course you are. I can only handle one of you. What's up?"

I could almost see Zane's shoulders squaring as he talked.

"I've learned a lot today, but right now I'm at the Maddison House. You'll never guess who just showed up?"

"Not that thing, or whatever it was, that we saw last night?"

I'll give him credit. He sounded strong, and not the least bit terrified. At least, that was one of us. He might be after he learned what we'd figured out, but right now was not the time to deal with that.

"No, worse. Well, relatively speaking, I guess. The Wonder Twins are here. Bernie said to ask if you could join us."

Zane didn't even hesitate.

"I'll be there in five minutes. I got off work early and was coming to see you. Don't engage with them, if you can."

"Yeah, that's not happening. They're bullying poor Norma right now. I'll see you when you get here. Zane?"

"Yes?"

"Thank you. For being there, I mean."

"Always. Keep the damage to a minimum before I get there, though, okay?"

"No promises," I said, signing off.

The warm fuzzy feeling I had when I first heard his voice stuck with me as I went down the stairs. It dissipated quickly when I saw Aiden and Jaden waving around a piece of paper in front of Norma.

"See, it says right here that we have authorization to be here. I need you to shut this place down and give us full access."

"What's going on?"

The twins turned to look at me, their handsome faces twisting into identical expressions of disgust.

"It's none of your business, that's what it is," Jaden said. "I'm sorry, but your design work is going to wait. What is happening here is way more important than some silly wallpaper."

I wasn't a huge fan of some wallpaper, but this guy irritated me to no end.

"I don't see why you feel the need to bully a woman over whatever it is you're doing," I said, stepping closer to Norma. "Let's use our words and our inside voices, okay, boys?"

Aiden's eyes flashed with something dark before he pasted on a grin that I'm sure made women swoon all over the place. Fortunately, it had zero power over me.

"Now, let's not get off track here," he said, smoothly. "I'm so sorry if you feel that we're being bullies. That's certainly not our intent. We just don't like it when people try to gate-keep."

"That's literally her job," I said, folding my arms over her chest. "Why are you here?"

"Yes, I'd like to know that, too," Russ Givens said, joining us. "I was on a call when I heard the disturbance. What's happening?"

"That seems to be the million dollar question," I said. "Jaden, do you care to explain?"

Jaden oozed his way towards us, flashing a fake grin.

"Mr. Givens, it's so nice to see you again. The last time we were here, you almost had us thrown out. We had to go over your head. We contacted the board of trustees that oversees the museum. If you'll look at this document, you'll see we're allowed to film."

He ripped the sheet away from Aiden and shoved it towards Russ, who took it like it might have carried the plague. I watched Russ's face as he read through the letter, and when he paled, I knew we were in trouble.

"I see," he said, folding it in half. "I'm afraid we were not informed of this. If you'll excuse me, I need to speak with Norma."

He pulled the older woman to the side, and I followed. The twins were sporting triumphant grins as they called to the rest of their crew, who must have been standing outside.

"Bring it all in, guys. Let's get this show on the road."

Men began carrying in cameras and lights, and boxes of what I assumed to be their equipment. I focused back on Russ and Norma.

"Sir, I don't understand it," Norma said, wringing her hands together. "This is all highly irregular."

"All I can think is that the board felt the publicity would be good for the museum. Maybe they're right," Russ said, looking over Norma's shoulder at the chaos. "I don't think we have much choice but to accept it. Go get your things and head home. I'll see what I can do."

I pulled Russ aside as Norma went behind the counter to grab her purse. She looked defeated, and that emotion was naked on Russ's face.

"There's nothing you can do?" I asked.

He shook his head and tried to smile.

"I'm afraid not. That document is legit. Even if I called the sheriff, they don't have to leave."

"The board must be out of their minds. These guys are frauds."

Russ gently clapped me on the shoulder and shrugged.

"It's best if we let them do their thing. Have you learned anything since we talked?"

"A lot. Enough to know that we're dealing with something way too serious for this crew of amateurs. Someone could get hurt."

Russ's face blanched, and he heaved a sigh.

"Well, let's hope that doesn't happen. I'm going to go home and see if I can get a few of the board members to talk to me. Maybe I can get them to change their minds."

His shoulders were slumped as he joined Norma. They walked out the door and seconds later, Zane appeared. He zeroed in on me and walked over, wrapping an arm around my waist.

"Is everything okay?"

"Who's this guy?" Aiden asked, looking over at us with interest.

"I'm Zane Matthews with Matthews Security. Who are you?"

"Oh geez," Jaden said, rolling his eyes. "Look, Mr. Rent-a-Cop, we've got authorization to be here. I don't know what the manager here told you, but you're not kicking us out."

A man stepped past him, carrying an enormous light, while running a cable behind him. The space was quickly filling up with their stuff.

"The manager didn't call me. I'm with Brynn."

"Oh good," Aiden said. "Maybe you can control her. She needs to get out of here and let us work."

Zane's eyes narrowed dangerously.

"Brynn is her own woman. I don't tell her anything. But if anyone messes with her, they answer to me."

Zane drew himself up to his full height while Jaden took a step back and raised his hands.

"Hey, man, we don't want to fight. Sorry if we irritated your girl-friend. We're just trying to do our jobs. We're having a seance tomorrow, and we need to get everything set up. It's going to take all night to get everything ready for tomorrow."

"You can't do that," I said, rushing over to stand next to Zane. "It's not safe."

"What?"

I instantly felt like an idiot and cursed myself for opening my big mouth. However much I didn't like these guys, though, I didn't want them to get hurt.

"I know the place is haunted. I also know there's something bigger than you know tied up in all of this. You don't know what you're messing with."

"Oh, that's priceless," Aiden said, making a face. "The interior designer thinks she knows about ghosts. How precious is that?"

"She's more than that," Zane said. "She's dealt with more than you charlatans could ever dream of. If she says it's not safe, it's not safe."

"Um, we're the real deal. We can handle whatever comes," Jaden said, sneering as he looked over at me. "I don't care what you think. It's obvious you're just a wanna-be. This is going to be huge. We'll have to air this episode during sweeps week. It's going to make a killing."

Bernie head-butted my leg, startling me.

"You can't let this happen. They'll be slaughtered. I'm not kidding."

"Look, I know we got off on the wrong foot," I said, glancing at Aiden and trying my best to be conciliatory. "Okay, maybe several wrong feet. I'm serious, though. A seance is a terrible idea."

"Awww, she brought her kitty cat with her again. How weird are you, lady? Maybe you should be locked up."

Zane growled and stepped in front of me, but I put my hand on his arm.

"You know what? Fine. Have your seance. I'm coming to it, though, and you can't stop me."

Oh geez. Why did I just say that? I bit my tongue, but it was way too late to take it back.

"The more the merrier, I always say," Jaden said, his voice dripping with disdain. "It will be a chance to prove you wrong. In case you're wondering, we'll be holding it at eight tomorrow. I doubt you'll show up, though. Little girls like you should be home taking care of their man."

I gritted my teeth and glared at the twins before turning to my cat. Bernie gave me a long look and nodded sharply. I guess a seance with a soul-hungry wraith was in our very near future. I was so not prepared for this. Zane took my hand and turned towards the twins.

"We'll both be there."

"I'm coming too," Bernie said, growling.

I knew what that meant to Zane, and my heart thumped hard in my chest. He'd already had a close brush with this entity, and he still had my back. I don't know how I ever deserved this man, but he was amazing. Even though I knew they couldn't understand Bernie, knowing he would help made me relax. A fraction, anyway.

"Fine. Bring everyone you want. They'll be amazed at what real ghost hunters can do, especially if they think you're legit."

He snorted and went back to setting up his equipment. I glanced at the box, noticing what looked like a frequency monitor.

I scooped up Bernie with my free hand and the three of us headed for the door. I wasn't sure what I'd signed us all up for, but in a little over twenty-four hours, we were going to find out.

13

The drive from Deadwood back to my house took only a few minutes, but it felt like an hour as I listened to Bernie tell me all the reasons that this was a very horrible idea. When he finally ran out of steam, I glanced over at him and tried to smile.

"I don't know what came over me, buddy. I just felt like if it was going to happen, I needed to be there. I didn't mean to say anything, but it just popped out."

Bernie sighed sharply and shook his little head.

"I know. I agree."

"Hey, if you agree, what was with that lecture?"

"Just because I agree it's necessary doesn't mean that it's smart. I don't want to encourage you to go jumping headlong into dangerous situations."

"That's kind of been my thing for the last few months."

"And that's the reason I'm getting gray whiskers."

I glanced at his muzzle and narrowed my eyes when I saw his whiskers were just as black as they'd always been.

"Hardee har har. So, what do we do now?"

"First, you need to park the car. Second, I'm hungry. Third, we need to create a plan of action that will help lessen the odds of you getting seriously hurt."

"Wait. Lessen? Shouldn't that be eliminate the odds?"

"I can only do so much."

His voice was serious and made the lump in my throat get even bigger. I'd never been involved in a seance, but I thought I knew the basics. On second thought, I'd really only seen it in movies, which meant I needed to get my rear into gear and do some research.

Zane pulled to a stop behind my car and we walked up to the steps together. He was quiet as we walked inside and I got Bernie's food dished up. I didn't know what to say, but I knew a hug would go a long way towards expressing what I was feeling inside. I wrapped my arms around his toned middle while he rested his chin on the top of my head.

"I'm really sorry I jumped in like that," I said after a few seconds. "I don't know why I said it, but there's no taking it back now. If you don't want to go with me, I completely understand."

Zane stepped back and raised my chin with a finger. I was almost afraid to see what was reflected in his eyes, but the pure love I saw there took me by surprise.

"I will always go where you go," he said. "No matter where that is, I'll be there. We're in this together."

A tear worked its way down my cheek and he rubbed it away with his thumb before kissing the spot. Bernie made a loud smacking noise from the kitchen, breaking the mood, and forcing us both to laugh. I looked over at my cat, and I'm pretty sure he winked at me before returning to his feast.

"So, what do we do?" Zane asked. "I'm pretty new to this paranormal thing."

"I guess we should research what is involved in a seance and how to do one properly. Something tells me the twin power tools don't know what they're doing. I'd hate for them to call up a demon from the deep or something."

Zane's eyes widened, and I held up a hand before continuing.

"I'm kidding."

I really hoped I was kidding. Who knew what could happen? I pulled out my laptop and opened it while Zane joined me at the kitchen table. By the time I'd typed in how to perform a seance into my search engine, Bernie jumped on the table and gave me an incredulous look.

"Are you seriously googling how to do a seance?"

"Well, yeah. I don't know how to do one. This seemed a logical place to start."

"You're going to rely on the collective people of the internet to teach you how to perform a complicated ritual that could go completely wrong?"

"Well, if you put it like that..." I said, trailing off. "What should I do?"

Bernie nuzzled my hand, purring softly, and turned his green eyes to mine.

"I'll take care of that part. You need to be careful and surround yourself with people who love you. This guy here is only one piece of the puzzle. He's a sizeable piece, but you need more backup."

Zane's eyebrow went up as he watched us communicate, and I hurriedly translated.

"I think that's a great idea," he said, nodding. "Give Logan a call and tell him we'll buy him dinner tomorrow afterwards. If I know anything about Logan, he'll agree to anything if there is food involved."

I couldn't help but snort. He wasn't wrong.

"Sounds good to me. Bernie, who else should we invite? I don't know many people and my parents are in Arizona."

Bernie was quiet for a second before nodding decisively.

"Logan will want to bring Kelsie, which should be okay. She's put aside her envy of you and she's grown a lot."

"Wait, when was she ever envious of me? I was the nerdy weirdo in school and she was the perfect one who could do no wrong."

"You were also the one with a loving and supportive family, something she never had," Bernie said. "That was an enormous force behind the way she treated you back then. She's over it now and you've both grown as people."

Oh. I'd never thought of it like that before. I was tempted to take a quick trip down memory lane, but that would have to wait.

"What about Sophie?" Zane asked when I went quiet. "You two are so close."

"If she'd be willing, I think that's a great idea," Bernie said. "She's the one who found the missing piece of information we needed about the wraith angle."

That reminded me Zane had a lot of catching up to do. I guess I knew what I was going to be doing this evening.

"Bernie recommended Kelsie, and you recommended Sophie. So, that's settled," I said. "Let's order in some food since someone, namely me, hasn't been grocery shopping, and we can work out a plan."

"Pizza?" Zane asked, whipping out his phone.

"I will literally never say no to pizza."

While Zane was ordering, my phone rang, and I glanced at the screen, surprised to see Bob Tremaine's name. I walked into the kitchen and hit accept.

"Hi, Bob. What's up?"

"I'm glad I caught you. I just got word of a house in Coppertown that might be perfect for what you're looking for. It needs a lot of work, but it fits your budget."

"Really? When can I see it?"

"Does tomorrow morning work? There's no one living there right now, so first thing should be a problem."

"That's great. I'll meet you there at eight. Thanks, Bob."

"I'll text you the address. See you then."

I ended the call and walked back over to the table and sat in front of my computer as I waited for Bob's text. Even with everything going on, the chance to put my plan into action for Reginald and Mimi, the couple who'd worked for the Graffs, filled me with excitement.

"Who was that?"

"Bob Tremaine. He's got a house he wants to show us for the Millers tomorrow at eight."

Zane's eyes sparkled as he grinned at me. He knew how important this was to me.

"That's fantastic. I've got to be at a meeting with that new client at eight, though," Zane said, deflating a little.

"Oh. Well, I'll take pictures and a video with my phone so we can decide together."

"It's your money, Brynn. You've got the final say," Zane said. "But I'd love to see it."

I waved my hand as my phone dinged with a text from Bob. I quickly typed in the address into my search bar and smiled when the first result showed a beautiful little cottage.

"Here it is. Oh my gosh, I can't believe the price!"

We went through the exterior pictures together and my heart rose as I thought about what we could do to it to make it a home for the lovely older couple. There weren't any pictures of the interior, which could mean that the insides were in awful shape. But, if that was true, the amount of work needed meant the price had to be negotiable, which would leave me plenty of money left over to make it nice.

"It looks perfect."

"Well, if it's half as good as it looks online, I'll probably put an offer in."

"You should see if Logan could go with you. He can look at the structural integrity and you can ask him about the seance while you're there."

The mention of the seance brought me back to earth with a sharp thud. As exciting as the prospect of finding a house was, my first order of business was to figure out this wraith thing and how to handle the twins.

"Good point. I'll text him and see what he says."

While I was typing out a text to Logan, my doorbell rang and Zane hopped up to answer it. I sent the text and Logan replied instantly with a thumb emoji. I debated calling Sophie, but it was getting late and I didn't want to bother her. I made a mental note to call her in the morning and joined Zane in the kitchen to help dish out the food.

Bernie followed me and sat at my feet, sniffing the air.

"I'll save you a piece of cheese."

There was little Bernie enjoyed more than a pinch of cheese from a fresh pizza. I snagged a piece of pepperoni from my slice on the way back to the table and munched on it while I moved my laptop.

"Tell me about your day," Zane said, "Besides the whole twins thing. Geez, they're not very nice."

I grimaced before shaking my head. What I had to say could wait until after we were done eating.

"Why don't you go first? My stuff can wait until we're not eating."

Zane's expression was a twin of mine, but he gave me a good-natured smile before he started talking about his new client.

"By the way, he wants to move forward with hiring you to do the interior design work. Maybe after all of this is wrapped up, you can make an appointment with him? I'll give you his contact information."

"That would be great! I feel like my skills are getting rusty. Lately, I've been so focused on ghosts, I haven't been working. The Graff job was basically moving stuff around."

"Well, you'd have a clean slate with this home. He wants to talk to Logan, too."

"I'll tell him about it tomorrow. If you have the address, I can do some research on it ahead of time. I enjoy gathering design ideas before I meet with a client. Thanks for doing this."

"It's nothing," Zane said, finishing his slice. "Besides, it means we can work together and there's nothing I like more than that. Everything is going to be taken down to the studs so I can run my security system wires. The guy is a little different, but he's okay."

It wasn't a ringing endorsement, but I wasn't kidding when I said I needed to do some design work. The payment Stephen Graff gave me was being saved to purchase the Miller's a house, and I hadn't had a paying client since the job I'd completed at the hotel where Kelsie worked.

We cleaned up our dishes and while we worked, I told Zane about what Sophie discovered. His eyebrows flew up as I talked about wraiths and their strange life expectancy, but I had to give him credit. He rolled with the punches. Bernie hopped up on the island and leaned against Zane's arm. I finished my story and dried my hands, turning so I could see his expression.

He looked thoughtful as he stroked Bernie's back.

"It sounds interesting," he said, finally. "Whatever it is, you've got me and this guy to watch your back. We'll figure it out."

His positivity warmed my soul. Even though we were about to face something that had the potential to be terrifying, I felt stronger knowing we were all in this together.

14

Somehow, despite everything that was going on, I slept. Hard. I woke up early, refreshed, and crept out of bed so I wouldn't wake Zane. Bernie padded softly behind me, yawning widely, as he followed me to the kitchen.

I dished up his food before making coffee and leaned against the counter while I waited for my brain juice to brew. It didn't take long for Zane to join me. He looked like a male model, standing there in his boxer shorts, hair adorably mussed. Why is it that men get to look so good waking up, while I resembled a creature from a low-budget horror movie? Sometimes, life just isn't fair.

"Good morning, sunshine," Zane said, pressing a kiss to my cheek before he smoothed my curly mop.

"Did you sleep well?"

"I did. How about you? No crazy dreams?"

"No. When I woke up, I almost couldn't believe it. I think the coffee's ready. You can have the first cup."

That right there said a lot about how I felt about Zane. Typically, nothing came between me and my coffee.

"Tell you what, we'll split it while we wait. Are you excited about seeing the house?"

"I can't wait. I already have tons of plans brewing in my head, but I'll have to see the inside first before I get too far ahead of myself. The exterior pictures were awesome, though. I think this might be the one for Reginald and Mimi."

"What if they decide to move, though?" Zane asked.

He had a point. The former butler and his wife had no children, so it wasn't like they were tied to this area.

"I guess I don't know. Well, if that happens, the house will be theirs and they can turn around and sell it."

"It's a really cool thing you're doing, Brynn," Zane said, taking a sip of his mug and passing it to me.

"I don't know about that. I just can't imagine working for someone your entire life, only to find out you've been turned out on the street. I understand why Stephen Graff gave his estate to charity, but I wish he'd made more provisions for Reginald and Mimi."

"You're the sweetest person," Zane said, turning my chin towards him. "Many people would have taken that fifty grand and splurged on themselves. It says a lot about you."

My cheeks heated, and I desperately wanted to change the subject. The Graff job had been one of the strangest I'd ever taken on. I still didn't quite know what to think of it.

"I can't wait to sketch out some design ideas," I said, filling another mug with coffee and topping off Zane's. "It kind of reminds me of my house."

Zane looked around the kitchen and nodded his head.

"The homes here are old, but you made this one feel spacious and full of light. You've definitely got a gift."

I smiled before sipping my coffee. I was proud of my little one-bedroom cottage. Sure, it was small, but I'd poured my heart into the place and made it my own. Shortly after graduation, I'd purchased the house with my money, and my dad, his brother, and Logan had helped make my dream a reality.

"Thanks. I love this place."

"I love it, too. When I walk in, it feels like you. Bright, cheerful, and full of love."

Tears pricked at the backs of my eyes when I saw his expression. Bernie saved me from blubbering like a fool by rubbing on my leg to get my attention.

"I'd like to go with you this morning," Bernie said, sitting at my feet.

"Sure, bud," I said, leaning over to rub behind his ears. "I'd better go get ready. I'll be out in a few."

I stood on my tiptoes to kiss Zane on the cheek, and zipped through my shower, full of excitement. Once I was dressed, I found Zane in the kitchen with a few takeout bags.

"Hey, where did all of that come from?"

"Online ordering is a beautiful thing. I figured we had time for a quick breakfast and wanted to treat you."

"Oh, my. Is this from that little bakery in town? I've been wanting to try it."

"It is," Zane said, taking a giant blueberry muffin out of a bag and handing it to me. "I remembered you saying that. I got us each a little something."

I bit into the muffin, closing my eyes, as the flavors washed over my tongue. There was a hint of lemon zest that made my taste buds sing in delight as I chewed.

"This has to be the best muffin on the face of the earth," I said, before taking another bite. "What did you get?"

"This one is double chocolate. Want a bite?"

We shared our muffins and I couldn't resist peaking into the remaining bags, where I found a couple scones and a few danish. Heaven, I tell you.

"I'll have to save these for later. That muffin was enormous. Thank you for doing this," I said, pinching off a little crumb for Bernie.

He took it delicately and closed his eyes, much like I had. Yep, this bakery had three new regular clients.

"Anything for my girl. And Bernie. I'd better get ready and head out for my meeting. We're going over some different options for this guy's security system. He wants the works."

I cleaned up while Zane showered and by the time he was done, Bernie hopped into his bag, looking at me expectantly.

"I'm coming, buddy. Just a few minutes."

He got comfortable, kneading at his lining, while Zane came into the kitchen. His long hair was still damp and my breath caught in my chest as he gave me a grin.

"I'll come back up here with plenty of time to spare so we can get ready. Is there anything special I need to do for the seance?"

That brought me back to earth with a thump. In my excitement over the house, I'd stowed thoughts about the seance in the back of my brain.

"I don't know," I said, glancing over at Bernie. "I guess we'll figure it out as we go. Thank you for agreeing to do this. I know it's difficult."

Zane pulled me into a hug, his warmth washing over me like a comforting blanket.

"That just means it's worth it. I'd do anything to keep you safe. Let me know what you think about the house. I can't wait to see your pictures and videos."

He kissed me gently and leaned his forehead against mine, before grabbing his bag and heading to the door.

"Later, Matthews," I said, finding my breath again.

"Later, Sullivan."

"Can we go now?" Bernie said, his tone only mildly annoyed. "You two are just too sweet for words."

I chuckled as I grabbed his bag and went to my car. Leave it to Bernie to keep me grounded. The drive to Coppertown only took a few minutes, and I pulled in behind Logan's pickup at the house. He was leaning against the driver's door and waved as I walked up with Bernie's bag.

"What's good, freckles?"

I rolled my eyes and elbowed him in the ribs before turning to look at the house. My first impression was that the photographer who'd been hired to take the exterior pictures was extremely gifted. In the morning light, the house looked a little on the dilapidated side, but I could see it had excellent lines.

"Thanks for meeting me here. What do you think of the place?"

Logan made a face and shrugged his shoulders as we walked up to the place. The yard was overgrown, and the stairs had a decided lean, but my mind was already imagining the possibilities. I set Bernie's bag down and opened the zipper for him. He raced out and disappeared around the side, intent on something.

"Is it okay for him to run around like that? The house? It's old. But if it's got good bones, that won't matter. When's Bob coming?"

I checked my watch and looked down the road, where I saw Bob's truck coming around the corner.

"Bernie will be fine. He always does this. There's Bob, now. I can't wait to see inside."

"How have things been?" Logan asked, looking at my face closely. "Is everything okay?"

I should've known I couldn't hide anything from my cousin. We'd known each other our whole lives.

"It's fine. Don't let me forget to ask you something later."

"Well, that's not a loaded statement or anything," Logan said, elbowing me as Bob approached.

"Good morning, you two," Bob said, extending his hand to Logan and then me. "Fine day, isn't it?"

"It is," I said, nodding. "It's still a little crisp, but I think it's supposed to warm up later."

"Ready to see the inside? I'll warn you, it's not in the best of shape, but with this price range, you already know what you're getting into."

"Let's see it," I said, as we followed him up the stairs.

They gave an alarming groan, but held, as the three of us entered the house. I blinked several times to let my eyes adjust and immediately focused on the beautiful wood trim that encircled the entryway. Sure, the plaster was full of holes, and there was trash piled up everywhere, but the woodwork was incredible. Bob led Logan down the hall while I stood in the living room and closed my eyes, trying to get a feel for the place as I took pictures and brief video clips for Zane.

I wasn't sure if it was part of my gift of being able to see ghosts, but I could always tell whether an old home had been a happy one, or a place of strife. Despite the current damage, it felt good. My heart soared as I walked around, noting the enormous windows and solid floor.

I went through the archway into the kitchen and looked up at the high ceilings. Yep, this place definitely had potential. Instead of the tiny kitchens that were sometimes found in these older homes, this one was huge. I closed my eyes and pictured Mimi cooking up her delicious meals to her heart's content.

If this house was structurally sound, I had a good feeling that it might be the one. I walked back through the living room and down the hall to where the bedroom was. It also needed new plaster, but once again, it was full of light.

"What do you think?" Bernie asked, appearing at my feet.

"Gah! How do you always do that?"

Bernie gave a kitty shrug and walked around the room.

"It's a gift. I like this place. I feel nothing bad about it."

"Me either. I think this might be the one. We'll have to see what Logan says."

"Talking to yourself again?" Logan asked as he joined us. "I think it needs a ton of work, but there's nothing wrong with the structure. I peeked into the crawl hole. It was clean, and the beams looked sound. Bob's waiting for us out front."

"I think you should buy it," Bernie said.

"Well, I guess that settles it. I'll put in an offer."

"I'll put together a budget," Logan said. "I wouldn't offer the listing price."

I shook my head as we walked back through the house.

"No, it needs a ton of work. The asking price is low, but I think there's some wiggle room."

We rejoined Bob on the lawn, where he was talking on the phone. I pulled Logan to the side while we waited.

"What's up?"

"I know it's not much notice, but would you be willing to go to a seance with me tonight at the Maddison House?"

"A what at the where?"

I took a deep breath and summed up what had been going on while my cousin listened intently. His face was drawn by the time I'd finished, but he nodded.

"You don't have to do it," I said, putting my hand on his arm.

"No, I'll be there. You need backup. I can't let the big lug you're dating get all the glory, can I?"

I rolled my eyes at his description of Zane. They'd had a rocky start when I first met Zane, but ever since then, they'd gotten along. Logan being Logan always had to get a dig in, though.

"Do you think Kelsie would want to go? I don't think either of you will be in any danger."

"She'll be there, especially once she hears it's for you. She's really changed, Brynn."

I smiled and gave him a quick one-armed hug.

"You've both been good for each other. It makes me happy."

"Hey, I'm perfect and not in need of changing," Logan said, puffing out his chest.

"Yeah, you keep telling yourself that."

Before he started dating Keslie, Logan was definitely a love them and leave them type of guy. Ever since they'd been reintroduced, I'd watched my cousin transform into a thoughtful, loving man, and the change was awesome. He didn't need to know that, of course, but I was proud of him.

Bob ended his call and joined us in front of the porch.

"What do you think?"

"I'd like to put in an offer. How flexible is the price?"

Bob looked at me and smiled, shaking his head.

"For you? I think I can get you an excellent deal. The seller has no attachment to the place. It used to be their aunt's house, and had been rented out for years. They don't want to pay to fix it up, and I think they just want to get rid of it. What are you thinking?"

I glanced at Logan before naming a figure well under the asking price. Bob nodded and reached his hand out for me to shake.

"I'll see what I can do and get back to you later today."

Bob walked back to his pickup, phone attached to his ear, as Logan and I walked back to our vehicles.

"So, what time do you need me to be at the Maddison House?" Logan asked.

Bernie darted past me as I opened the door and he scrambled into the passenger seat.

"Eight. Be a little early, though. I'm going to ask Sophie if she'll join us."

"Oh cool, I haven't seen her in ages. Does she still work at the library?"

"She does. You should go in more often."

"Yeah, yeah. See you later, carrot top."

I stuck my tongue out at him as I got into my car. I put the key in the ignition, but took another look at the house. I couldn't believe we'd found a place for the Millers. I sent some pictures to Zane before pulling away from the house. I wanted to ask Sophie in person, and by the time I got back to Deadwood, the library would be open.

15

*a*s I found a parking spot in front of the library, I felt a strong case of déjà vu. I checked on Bernie, who was napping in his bag, and decided not to wake him. I eased out of my seat and quietly shut the door before heading down the walk towards the library.

The sun was out, but the day hadn't yet warmed up, so I pulled my hoodie sleeves down over my hands as I walked. While I loved Fall, I wasn't looking forward to the cold and snow. However, I suppose that meant that cozy snow days with Zane were in my future, which was definitely something to look forward to.

I walked into the library and felt a rush of relief as I saw Sophie behind the desk, looking as fit as ever. She grinned when she saw me and rushed around the desk to give me a hug.

"I was so sorry I missed you yesterday. Stacia told me you came in. Did you get my note?"

"I did, and thank for you finding the piece of the puzzle we were missing," I said, glancing around to make sure Stacia wasn't within hearing distance. "I think you're right that we're dealing with a wraith."

"Speak freely, dear. It's just me this morning. Stacia isn't coming in until this afternoon."

She walked back behind the desk and took a seat while I leaned on the counter and told her everything I'd learned so far. I left nothing out, even my interactions with the twins. Her face screwed up when I got to the part about them bypassing Russ and getting permission from the board to film inside.

"I sure hope they break nothing in that museum with their hijinks."

"That's a good word you don't hear every day."

"Well, it should be used more often. I've found it quite apt in many situations."

I laughed softly as I watched my friend. She looked okay, but I couldn't help but worry about her. I didn't want to pry, but I had to know. Especially if I was going to ask her to take part in a seance.

"Stacia mentioned you were at the doctor's office. Is everything okay?"

Sophie waved an elegant hand, her many bracelets jingling, and beamed at me.

"I'm perfectly fine. I should've known you'd worry. It was nothing more than my annual checkup. I'm happy to report I'm fit as a fiddle. In fact, the doctor said I'm healthier than most people half my age."

The tension I'd been storing melted away as she talked. Sophie took excellent care of her health, exercised constantly, and had been a vegetarian for years.

"I'm so glad to hear that. Speaking of doctors, I should probably have an annual check-up, too. Or, I guess at this point it would be a triennial exam."

She narrowed her eyes and shook her finger at me playfully.

"Don't put it off. You'll be glad you went in. So, what are you planning to do about the Ghost Twins?"

I made a face and rested my chin on my hand.

"They're insisting on holding a seance, and you know how I am. I volunteered to be a part of it."

"Oh! How exciting! I've always wanted to take part in something like that. You know how I love hearing your stories. Do you think I might see a ghost if I went?"

I shrugged my shoulders, not knowing the answer.

"I guess it could be possible. That's why I'm here. I wanted to see if you wanted to go with me. Zane is coming, as are Logan and Kelsie."

"Well, count me in. What time do I need to be there?"

"Eight, but we're all coming a little early. Are you sure you want to?"

"I wouldn't miss it for the world. My very first seance. I'm so excited. Is there anything I should bring?"

"I don't think so. Be prepared, though. The twins are something else."

"Oh, I think you know I have a lot of experience dealing with people. I run a tight ship here at the library and I don't put up with any guff."

She smiled widely, and I couldn't help but notice the sparkle in her eye. Hearing about the seance really seemed to perk her up and suddenly, I was very glad I'd asked her. I knew Bernie would do everything in his power to keep the people I loved safe, and having her with me meant everything.

"That settles that then. I'll see you at the Maddison House later today."

"I just know the rest of the day is going to drag by now," she said, heaving a dramatic sigh. "It will be a lesson in patience."

"Patience is a virtue."

She snorted, and we both broke into laughs. Seeing my friend made my heart feel about ten pounds lighter, and I felt like I was no longer dreading the seance. There was something to be said about surrounding yourself with the people you love.

"See you later, dear," Sophie said, coming around the desk for another hug. "I can hardly wait."

I walked back outside and joined Bernie in the car. He awoke as I slid in and blinked at me like a befuddled owl for a second before yawning hugely.

"Big yawn!"

I swear he rolled his eyes at me, but it might have been a trick of the light. I pulled onto the road and headed for home.

"How was Sophie?" Bernie asked, stretching so hard the passenger seat shook a little.

"Great. She's on board for tonight."

"Good," he said, nodding. "We need to go home and begin our preparations."

"What preparations? What are we going to need to do? I really know nothing about this."

"You'll learn. Before you go home, we need to hit up that crystal shop."

"I wish you'd said something earlier," I said, looking for a driveway where I could turn around. "Where is the shop? I didn't even know we had one in town."

"It's on the outskirts, on the opposite side. I have a list of things that will be useful and I have a feeling we should go there."

I backtracked through town until I found the crystal shop Bernie wanted. It was a newer store, and I'd yet to visit it. Once I found a place to park, my cat rattled off my shopping list.

"Oregano?" I asked, breaking into his flow. "Are we making spaghetti?"

"Focus, Brynn. Everything doesn't have to be about food."

"Says the cat, who can't go over three hours without a snack."

"I have greater needs than the average cat. I'll have you know..."

"Yes, I know. You're not an average cat. What are you, by the way?"

"Besides oregano, I'll also need a good amount of dill, parsley, and lavender."

"Sounds like I could've gone to the grocery store."

"These need to be dried and in their complete form, smarty pants. Are you writing this down?"

I grabbed my phone and started making a list, typing as fast as my fingers could go as he kept talking.

"Okay, so some cheesecloth, glass bottles, and olive oil. I hope you know what you're doing," I said, finishing the list.

The look he shot me made me bite my lip to keep from laughing. He looked so adorably fierce I couldn't help but lean over and give him a kiss on the top of his fuzzy little head. His answering purr told me he wasn't that mad at me, and I smiled as I got out of the car.

"I'll be back in a flash."

"Don't forget the salt! It's very important."

I shut the door and double checked my list to ensure I hadn't forgotten his precious salt. I walked into the shop and took a deep breath as the smell of incense wafted over me.

"Greetings, fellow traveler," the girl behind the counter said.

Her hair was dyed a combination of purple, teal, and vibrant blue, giving the effect of a magical mermaid. Her eye makeup echoed those tones, and I almost felt like I'd tumbled into another plane as we looked at one another.

"Um, hi. I need to get a few things, but I'm not sure you have them in stock."

"I hope we have everything you will need, my sister," she said, spreading her hands wide. "If not, I can point you in the right direction."

Her serene smile put me at ease and I handed over my phone with Bernie's list. She read through everything and cocked an eyebrow at me.

"You are about to do something dangerous."

"How do you know that?"

"Everything on this list should repel bad spirits. It's none of my business," she said, waving her hand. "But I can make a few other recommendations if you're open to suggestion."

"Sure, why not?"

I figured the more the merrier was definitely the theme of the day. She walked behind the counter, her long skirt swishing over her bare toes, and snagged a wicker basket with a rope handle.

"I'm Mallory Moon," she said, flashing me a smile over her shoulder as she began adding my items to the basket.

"Brynn Sullivan. It's nice to meet you."

"How long have you seen ghosts?"

She threw out the question so off-handedly I answered without thinking.

"Since I was three, I think."

"Interesting. It is a gift that must be a heavy burden. I don't share it, but I've known people who have."

She looked into my eyes and it felt like she was seeing into my soul. I blinked, startled, and nodded without thinking.

"It can be. But it's worth it."

"Your aura confirms that. It's a beautiful pink that deepens to a ruby red at your center. You're very strong. Don't forget that."

"I... I guess I won't. Thank you."

She waved her hand and placed a large bag of salt in the basket. Her eyebrows furrowed as she looked at me.

"No thanks are needed. I call things as I see them. You have a battle in front of you. I wish I could offer more, but I will think of you tonight while you make your stand. I feel you will be victorious, but it will not be easy. Remember your heart."

Her expression lightened as she moved over to a selection of crystals and began poking around.

"What are you looking for?"

"Black Tourmaline. It protects from negative thoughts. I think it will be very useful. You struggle with that, no?"

I wasn't sure what to make of Mallory Moon, but so far, she'd been spot-on. I chewed on my lip before nodding.

"I do."

She stopped at the pink crystals that were hanging from leather cords and picked one, sliding it over my head.

"There. I think that will be everything."

She swept past, back to the register, and began ringing everything up. I mentally checked off the things that were on my list and confirmed I hadn't forgotten everything. She tucked everything into a brown paper sack and tied the top with a beautiful ribbon.

"Thank you for your help. I appreciate it."

"Any time. Please, come in again. Next time, bring your helper with you. I have a feeling he would enjoy this place."

I blinked, surprised, before a big smile spreading across my face.

"I will. It was nice meeting you."

"It was. I've met no one of your abilities here. I think we will have much to discuss once you have completed your task."

I waved before walking outside, feeling absurdly light hearted. As I got closer to my car, I couldn't help but wonder if Bernie had engineered my coming here. I opened the door, and he looked at me with his whiskers quirked as I sat down.

"Did you find everything?"

"Everything you mentioned and more," I said, fastening my seat belt and stowing the bag behind my seat. "I think you knew about the more part."

"I had a sense the owner of this establishment would be helpful."

"Her name's Mallory Moon. She said to bring you in next time."

"Excellent. I've been running low on a few things. I'm glad to see she is legit. One never knows."

"No, one doesn't, does one?" I said, tucking him under the chin before I pulled out of my parking space. "Do we head home now?"

"Yes, we've got some work to do before eight. And I need food. And a nap."

"Yes, my liege."

I steered home, wondering what we were going to do with all these herbs and things. I pressed the rose quartz necklace to my chest as I drove, noticing it felt warm against my skin. While the seance was looming in the back of my mind, I had a feeling that everything was going to be okay. Somehow.

16

*B*y the time Zane came to pick me up a little before seven, I'd spent the rest of my day making sachets, herb infused oils, and taking directions from Bernie. I wasn't sure who was more tired, but the two of us were a sight as Zane walked in.

He sniffed the air and looked at my disheveled hair, eyebrows cocked.

"It smells like you've been making spaghetti, but I don't see any food. Is everything okay?"

I nodded, grimacing when I realized my pony tail was flopped to one side.

"We're fine. I made a new friend at the crystal shop and spent the rest of the day getting pushed around by my cat. Everything is fine."

Bernie mumbled something about if he only had opposable thumbs he wouldn't need to put up with substandard help, but I ignored him. Zane approached me and wrapped me into a much needed hug.

"That's great. You made a friend. What's her name?"

"Mallory Moon. She's pretty cool."

"That can't be her real name?"

I waved my hand and finished gathering up all of our supplies into a box that I'd salvaged from the trash.

"Probably not, but she has the best mermaid hair I've ever seen, and she can see auras."

"Okay... So, what's the plan, my dear?"

I blew my hair off my forehead and looked at my herb stained hands.

"I'm going to get cleaned up and then we can head to the museum. Sophie, Logan, and Kelsie are going to meet us there."

Zane's expression cleared, and I realized I should have led with that. He must have been worried it would only be the two of us.

"That's good. How was the house?"

I bounced in place and shot him a grin before walking down the hall.

"I'll tell you while I get ready. It's amazing. I'm so excited about it."

Zane listened patiently while I rambled on about how much I loved the little house Bob found as I wrestled my hair back into a ponytail and got washed up. I glanced at my clothes and turned to look at him.

"I think you look great. I'm not sure what you're supposed to wear to a seance, but I think comfort is probably important."

"You're right. There's no point in changing. Well, I think this is as ready as I'm going to get. Let's grab our stuff, and Bernie, and you can tell me about your day while we drive into town."

Zane helped me load the box containing our supplies into his Jeep, and Bernie reappeared, hopping into his carrier.

"You've got your necklace on and that stone with you, right?" Bernie asked.

"Yes. That's the fourth time you've asked, but I still have everything with me."

"It's only the second time, and it's important," Bernie said, letting out a wounded sniff.

"I'm sorry, bud. I'm all keyed up. Thank you for worrying about me. Is there anything you need? I want you to be safe, too. Maybe I should have gotten you something to tie around your neck."

"I'll be fine."

I grabbed his strap and looked up to see Zane leaning against the doorway, watching us with a bemused expression.

"I'm glad he worries about you," Zane said, taking my hand. "It makes me feel better knowing he's always watching over you."

"He's the best," I said, winking at Bernie through the mesh side of his carrier. "I'd be lost with him. You, too."

Bernie blinked at me and we headed to the Jeep. I looked at my house, feeling a sudden pang of homesickness as Zane pulled away. I'd never gone into something like this, and a part of me wondered if I'd ever see my little house again.

"It's going to be okay," Zane said, squeezing my head. "Don't worry so much."

"Shouldn't that be my line?"

Zane threw his head back and laughed, long hair brushing the tops of his shoulders. While we drove, he filled me in on what he'd talked about with his new client. The guy wanted everything to be top of the line, and it sounded like there might be more to the story. I cocked my head to the side and Zane nodded.

"Yeah. I think he's going to need more than just your design skills. I don't want to get too much into it before we go into the seance, but I think there's something really weird going on at his house."

"Maybe that's why he feels so paranoid. I can't wait to check it out."

The drive into Deadwood felt like it took seconds, and before I knew it, we were parked out front, where Sophie was talking to Logan and Kelsie. I took a deep breath and glanced over at Zane.

"Are you ready for this? We don't have to do it," Zane said, tucking a hair that had come out of my ponytail behind my ear.

"I think we do. I don't like the Ghost Twins, but I would hate for something to happen to them. Wraiths are serious and they could end up hurt, or worse. We've got to do this."

"Then let's get it done so I can take everyone out to a celebratory dinner. Something tells me we're going to need to refuel before the night is over."

My stomach picked that moment to let out a tortured growl, and Bernie huffed a laugh in the back seat.

"Now, who can't go three hours without a snack?"

"I know, we're a lot alike," I said, reaching back for his bag. "Let's do this."

Zane grabbed the box, and I walked up to Sophie, smiling at everyone. She was vibrating with excitement as she looked at us, clasping her hands together.

"There you are. I'm so nervous I don't know what to do with myself. How are you, Zane?"

He kissed her cheek, making her blush, and nodded at my cousin and Kelsie.

"Hello, Sophie. Hi Kelsie, Logan," Zane said, fist bumping my cousin.

"A fist bump will do. I don't need a kiss," Logan said, slapping Zane on the back.

Kelsie and I shared an eye roll as I lowered Bernie's bag to the ground.

"Thank you for coming, guys. It means a lot. I know this is going to sound really weird, but I have a few things for each of you and it's super important to keep them in your pockets during this seance."

I dug into the box Zane was carrying and passed out the sachets I'd made to everyone. The little bundles of fabric held all the herbs I'd purchased, and Bernie swore they would help protect everyone. Logan raised an eyebrow, but obediently tucked it into his pocket. Sophie took a sniff of hers, sneezing a little.

"Oh, that's an interesting combination. After we're done, I'd love to know the history behind the meaning of these herbs."

I nodded as I got the little bottle of oil out of the box and passed it to Kelsie.

"Definitely. So, with the oil, you're supposed to take a small amount and place it on your forehead. I know it smells a little powerful, but again, it should help keep you safe."

"I was just telling everyone what we're dealing with," Sophie said, nodding at Kelsie to put the oil on her head. "I think everyone is up to speed on wraiths."

Kelsie looked a little lost as she passed the bottle to Logan, but I had to hand it to her. She showed up.

"I really appreciate this, Kelsie. Since we've reconnected, it's been one thing after another."

She smiled and hooked her arm around mine.

"I'm here for you. I may not understand it, but I know you need us. We won't let you down."

Tears clogged suddenly in my throat as everyone finished their preparations. Somehow, I'd gone from having my cousin as my best, and only, friend, to being surrounded by people who put themselves on the line for me.

"What are you guys doing out here?" Aiden asked from the top of the steps, sneering down at us.

I took another deep breath and forced myself to meet his eyes without flinching. Something about him reminded me of a person Kelsie and I had known in school, and he pushed all my buttons.

"We're preparing for something very serious. I hope you and your team are also taking precautions."

"Whatever. If you're going to take part in the seance, you need to get in here. We've got everything set up, so make sure none of you rubes trips over anything."

Sophie pulled herself to her full height and somehow looked down her nose at Aiden, even though he was standing feet above us. I bit back a grin as she cracked her official librarian voice over his head.

"Young man, that is no way to speak to your elders. We will be there precisely when we need to be."

Aiden at least had the grace to look abashed as we all filed up the steps. I slung Bernie's bag over my shoulder and patted my pocket, reassuring myself that the black tourmaline was still stowed inside of it.

The interior of the museum had been transformed into what looked like a film studio. A ring of cameras was set up around a rug that was centered on the floor. Candles flickered on nearly every surface. I spotted Jaden and a few of the camera crew, talking amongst themselves as we entered.

"Finally. We thought you chickened out," Jaden said, his handsome face made ugly by the expression he was wearing. "Alright everyone, let's go."

I unzipped Bernie's bag, and he shot out like he'd been fired out of a cannon. I turned back to Zane and nodded at him to place the box he was carrying on the floor next to me.

Bernie had been clear about what I needed to do. I'd made enough sachets and oil for everyone, even if they weren't wanted. Once everyone was settled, I needed to create a circle with the salt I'd purchased. He'd stressed that it was vital that once the circle was drawn, no one was to break it. The camera crew would be outside of the circle, and hopefully safe. I cleared my throat to get everyone's attention.

"I know this seance is your deal, but I made a few protection items for everyone. If you'd like one, please take a sachet and place it in your pocket," I said, making eye contact with a few of the crew members.

They glanced between me and the twins. One man came forward and grabbed a sachet, sticking it into his pocket, before nodding at me and returning to his camera. The others scoffed and poked fun, but he shook his head and focused on his work.

Aiden strolled over and made a big show of taking out a sachet and smelling it.

"What the heck is this thing? It stinks."

"Protection herbs. You don't have to take it, but it wouldn't be a bad idea, just in case."

"I don't need this. I've done tons of seances without this stupid stuff. Come on, we need to get started," he said, tossing the sachet back into the box.

My friends arranged themselves on one side of the rug, leaving me a spot between Zane and Sophie. The twins took up their spots on the other side, and I grabbed the packet of salt and started walking in a circle.

"What are you doing now?" Jaden asked, giving me a strange look.

"I'm sprinkling a salt barrier to contain the spirit you're trying to call. It's vital that no one cross this circle once the seance begins."

"Oh geez, you're something else. I told you, we've done seances tons of times. Everyone sit down and join hands."

I ignored Aiden and completed the circle, finishing the bit behind where I would be sitting. I joined my friends and tried to get comfortable as I took Sophie and Zane's hands. Poor Zane and Logan got stuck holding the hands of the twins, but I was glad I wouldn't be touching either of them.

Someone in the crew flipped off the lights and the candles around the room wavered for a split second before returning to their warm glow. I took a cleansing breath as Bernie climbed into my lap. We'd agreed that he'd whisper directions to me if it was necessary. Knowing the twins, it was going to be necessary.

The red lights on the cameras flared to life, and I looked over at Jaden as he grinned widely and stared into a camera.

"Hello, everyone. We're here at the Maddison House, about to perform a special seance to contact a spirit. This is very dangerous, but you know nothing will stop us in our hunt for the truth. Watch, and be amazed."

Zane's hand gripped mine tighter, and I shook my head as Aiden and Jaden began chanting together. The words they were saying made little sense, but a wind picked up suddenly, startling me. I glanced over my shoulder as Bernie whispered in my ear.

"They have a fan over there."

The candles flickered as Aiden increased the volume of his chanting and I focused back on the center of the rug. At first, it seemed like the twins were faking it, but I felt Bernie stiffen in my lap as the temperature in the room dropped. It was show time.

The hair on the back of my neck stood up, and I gripped Sophie's hand a little tighter. She gave me a reassuring squeeze back.

Aiden and Jaden's chanting cut off as something swirled in the middle of the rug. They leaned closer to each other, murmuring.

"What the..." Jaden said, eyes wide. "Dude, what's going on?"

"I don't know. This has never happened before," Aiden said, his voice shaking. "What did you do?"

"I just did the same chant we always do. This wasn't supposed to happen. Cameras, are you rolling?"

"Yeah, boss. Nothing's showing up, though."

The temperature dropped further and the swirling ether in the middle of the room solidified. Red eyes flared to life at the center of the mist and I felt terror grip my chest like a vise.

"Dude... no way," Aiden said.

From the awe in his voice, it was clear he'd experienced nothing like this. I could feel the tension in both Sophie and Zane's arms as the feeling of terror notched up again. Something wasn't right.

Jaden's head slapped to the left suddenly, and he let out a screech. Even in the dim light, I could see his face redden where he'd been struck.

"Bro, make it stop," he said, looking at his brother.

"I thought you were doing this."

Aiden's face jerked to the other side, and a matching red mark appeared on his cheek. He bolted to his feet, and I looked up, terrified.

"Don't leave the circle," I said, shouting to be heard over the very real wind that picked up suddenly.

He ignored me, moving backwards. As his foot left the circle, a horrible keening noise filled the room, and it felt like we'd been thrust into a deep freeze.

"This isn't good," Bernie said. "Brynn..."

The candles all went out at the same time and I felt something grab me around the neck, squeezing tightly. My last conscious thought was of my friends as I struggled to breathe before I blacked out.

*a*s I blinked my eyes open, I heard a groaning next to me, and turned my head, trying to see through the dense fog swirling around me. Oh great, it looked like I'd been booked for another free trip to the ether. Remind me to fire my travel agent.

The mist thinned, and I saw a man lying next to me, his face turned away. I scrabbled onto my knees and touched his arm, wincing as he let out another groan. He turned his face towards me and I bit back a sigh. Of all the people that had to come with me to the ether, it had to be this guy.

"Where am I?" Aiden asked, blinking fast. "What is this place?"

I sat down and wrapped my arms around my knees, figuring it was better than pacing while I waited for whatever calamity was soon to be in store.

"Bernie calls it the ether. It's the space between."

"Oh, well, if your cat says so, I guess it has to be true. You talk like you belong in a bad fantasy movie. Obviously, I'm dreaming and my subconscious dragged you in here. I don't know why. I don't find you the least bit attractive."

"Um. Okay?"

"I mean, you're pretty and all, but that red hair has to go. Maybe you could dye it?"

"Look, you're not dreaming. This is an actual place. I've been here before. Some freaky things are about to go down and it's best if you're prepared for them. I'm guessing since you were the one to break the circle, you got sucked in after me."

Aiden struggled into a seated position and looked around him.

"This blows. What is this place?"

I sighed and pinched the skin on the bridge of my nose, debating on whether I should waste my breath explaining things to him. I figured I had nothing better to do, so I started talking about the wraith while I looked around for Bernie. He typically joined me here, and I was feeling decidedly vulnerable.

"And so, you somehow called the wraith, and then you did the one thing you were never supposed to do, and you broke the circle," I said, finishing up.

"How did I call the wraith? We were just saying some mumbo jumbo so that it looked good on camera. Typically, we turn on the fan and then use some dry ice to set the scene... I mean, I don't know what you're talking about. This is all your fault."

"Look, I already knew you were a pair of phonies. I've been able to see ghosts since I was three. Maybe you weren't the ones who called him, but he showed up. I guess maybe wraiths don't need an engraved invitation or a hokey seance to appear."

"Hey, we're not phonies. It's just good to set a scene. Bland footage doesn't sell, so we jazz up our scenes a little. It doesn't mean we're fake."

"You keep telling yourself that."

A howl sounded in the distance, cutting off my words, and the hair on the back of my neck stood up. It broke off with an anguished squeal and silence fell.

"That was odd," I said, pulling myself to my feet.

"You think?" He asked, his voice breaking and his eyes wild. "I've gotta get out of here."

He started backing away, and I held my hand up to stop him.

"It's probably best if we don't split up. Trust me, I don't exactly want your company, but I want you to stay safe."

The howl sounded again, much closer, and I froze in place, unable to move. From the look on Aiden's face as he struggled, he was in a similar predicament.

"Let me go!"

"I'm not doing this. We need to stay calm."

The howl gained in volume, threatening to burst my eardrums before cutting off as a creature wreathed in black appeared next to me.

"You," it said, dragging out the word.

It reached for me, and I rocked backward, held in place by my frozen feet. Crap on a cracker. I'd seen some crazy stuff, including a banshee, but this being took the cake. It looked like it was wearing a strange, filmy robe, made of blackness. The space where there should have been a face within the cowl was oddly blank, but the mist inside was moving alarmingly. I swallowed hard.

"I don't know what you mean. Are you Thomas Morrow?"

A thin squeal filled the air, and the cowl turned towards me. I tried not to look inside of it as the wraith drew closer. I closed my fingers around the black tourmaline in my pocket and gathered my courage.

"How do you know my name?" it asked, hissing.

"Research. I don't know what you have planned, or what you've done with William Maddison, or the other ghost, Peter, but you need to stop. I won't let you hurt Arabella. I think you've done enough to her already."

My words sounded braver than I felt, but I stood my ground while Aiden glanced between me and the wraith.

"What's going on?" Aiden asked.

The wraith hissed and drifted out of my reach. It circled Aiden, and the cowl lifted, as though it were sniffing him.

"Maybe this will end better than I thought," the thing that used to be Thomas Morrow said. "You'll do nicely. I didn't know you'd come when I pulled her to this side, but now I see. I see what I need to do."

That didn't sound good. Nope. Not good at all. I held out a hand and cleared my throat.

"Sorry, Mr. Wraith, but that will not happen. I mean, this guy is a tool, but I know what you have planned. Even he doesn't deserve that."

It rounded on me, hissing, and if my feet weren't frozen in place, I would have backpedaled.

"Silence, you fool. You've meddled enough. This is my world you're in."

"I don't think that's true. I'm guessing any second there's going to be an afterlife warden coming to collect you and take you where you belong."

It hissed and drew back before turning to Aiden. I had to do something, but I wasn't sure what.

"I searched for a form before my old one failed. It wasn't nearly as nice as this one. You will do nicely."

The wraith poked at Aiden's chest, while Aiden turned the color of curdled milk. A sheen of sweat slicked his brow, and he gave me a desperate look.

"No. I won't let you inhabit him. What did you do with the souls you took?"

It let out a raspy chuckle.

"They were delicious."

I swallowed hard, debating my next move, when a whisper caught my attention. I almost smiled when I heard Bernie's familiar voice echo in my head. Help was on the way.

"Distract him, Brynn. I'm coming."

"Why did you kill Arabella? What did that poor girl ever do to you?"

The wraith's cowl turned towards me again and it drifted closer, chuckling again. If I thought the screaming thing was bad, the chuckling was worse. Way worse.

"My sweet Arabella? I loved her from afar for so long. She was my perfect princess. Why didn't she let me love her? It was all her fault."

The wraith's sibilant tone took on a whine as it circled around me.

"Her fault? You like to play the blame game, don't you? She was a young girl who was alone in the world. She didn't feel the same about you and you killed her. Am I right? Why didn't you capture her soul when you killed her? Or weren't you a wraith yet?"

It turned its nightmare face to me and inched closer until the fabric of the cowl nearly touched my skin.

"Don't you think I tried? She got away. She took refuge where I couldn't go. I tried to get into the house, but they kept turning me away. I got caught sneaking into the basement and they had me arrested. I had to leave. Before I left, I told her I would be back for her. I spent the rest of my life studying and sharpening my skills until I could return for her. Don't you see? We should have been together, fused, for all eternity."

"That's not how it works," I said, tears running down my face. "I've seen what waits on the other side. The good place. The people you love wait for you until it's your time. It's the most beautiful thing possible. They don't hunt you down and absorb you. They don't kill people needlessly and steal their souls. Eternal life is real, but you've twisted it around. What you're attempting to do is a mockery, and I won't let you do it."

I could feel something building as the mist thickened around us. Slowly, ever so slowly, I felt my feet again. I inched one forward and nearly sobbed in relief as it moved.

"Brynn, do it now," Bernie said, shouting as he streaked towards me through the mist.

"Do what?" I said, panicking as the wraith started towards me.

"You know what to do!"

I faced the wraith and gulped hard, feeling my hands raise on their own. An idea flashed through my head and I grabbed the wraith's head, holding it between my hands. It struggled, caught, and began hissing. My entire being screamed at me to let go, but suddenly, I knew what I needed to do. Words came into my head, and I repeated them, unsure but willing to try.

"This ends here. Begone."

Slowly, ever so slowly, the blackness enveloping the wraith

faded away until I was left standing with my hands holding nothing. My chest hitched as I realized it was over. Somehow, I'd banished the wraith. I collapsed into a puddle and opened my arms as Bernie closed the final distance between us. Even though we were in the ether, I could feel his soft fur between my fingers. Tears flowed down my cheeks and I held him close, rocking back and forth.

"You did good, Brynn. I knew you could do it," Bernie said, licking my cheek with his raspy tongue.

"Whoa. He talks?"

I'd almost forgotten about Aiden until his grating voice reminded me he was still here.

"Yeah. He does. We need to go back now. I'd appreciate it if you, um, kept what you saw here to yourself."

He raised a shaky hand and raked it through his blond hair.

"I don't think anyone would believe me. I'm pretty sure this is a twisted up dream of some sort. I must have tripped over a camera and hit my head and I'm unconscious. Yeah, that makes way more sense than this."

I shrugged, willing to let him believe whatever he needed to. The mist thinned and suddenly, I couldn't feel Bernie anymore. I looked down at him, concerned, but he blinked his eyes slowly.

"Wake up, Brynnie. Please wake up."

It sounded like Logan's voice, but I wasn't sure. I glanced over at Aiden and watched in wonder as his form evaporated.

"Brynn, can you hear us?"

That was Sophie, I was sure of it. I looked down at Bernie, and he nodded.

"It's time. You've got to wake up. You shouldn't stay here longer than necessary," he said, fading from view.

"Brynn, come back to me. I can't take it if you leave. Please."

Hearing Zane's voice catch as he pleaded shook me to my core. I closed my eyes and the next thing I knew, I was looking up at the ceiling of the Maddison House, while my friends and Zane knelt over me. Bernie sat on my chest, staring at me.

"Sweetheart, you're back," Zane said, scooping me up and clasping to his chest as Bernie squiggled between us.

"It's okay, everything is okay," I said, my voice muffled by his shirt.

I could feel Sophie's hand on my back as Zane cradled me close. I wanted so much to ask Bernie what happened, but I knew this wasn't the right time. He squeezed out from between Zane and me and nodded, understanding.

"Let her stand," Logan said, brushing his hand over the back of my head. "I want to make sure she's okay."

"I'm fine, really," I said, as Zane stood, carrying me like a small child. "I can stand."

"Be careful," he said, lowering my feet as if they were made of glass.

Kelsie surprised me by stepping close and hugging me. She squeezed one more time before stepping back and looking into my eyes.

"I'm so glad you're okay. Brynn, I want you to know that…"

I gripped her arm and smiled.

"I understand. Thank you for being here."

Loud voices echoed through the room, and I looked over at where Jaden and Aiden were standing. I'd almost forgotten about them. They were shouting orders at their camera crew to get everything packed up. I shook my head and looked at my circle of friends.

"Who's hungry?"

Zane ran a hand through his hair, mussing it up, and laughed.

"Only you would say something like that. At least if you're hungry, you're okay."

"I'm fine. Honestly. I could really go for a steak, though. My treat, everyone."

Sophie threaded her arm around my waist and squeezed me gently.

"You terrified us. When things calm down, I'd love to know what happened," she said, looking over at the camera crew as they raced around the room.

"I'll tell you everything, I promise. Let's get out of here."

We picked our way through the mess of equipment and I grabbed Bernie's bag. He stayed close, lending his support, as I came to a stop in front of the twins. Aiden refused to meet my eyes and Jaden was too busy shouting orders to focus on us. Aiden stepped closer and leaned towards me.

"Are you leaving?" Zane asked, putting a protective arm around my shoulders while he glared at the twins.

Aiden nodded, still unwilling to look at me.

"Yeah, we'll be cleared out within the hour. The tip we got was bogus. There's nothing interesting in this place at all. Jaden's taking me to the ER to get checked out. I think I must have hit my head."

He finally made eye contact and what I saw there hurt my heart a little. He wasn't a nice guy. In fact, he was a pretty awful human being, but he didn't deserve to suffer through that horror. I patted his arm and smiled.

"It will be okay. Sometimes dreams have a funny way of disappearing without a trace."

I prayed that would be true for him as I followed my friends out into the moonlight. The night air was crisp as we headed to our vehicles. I looked up at the Maddison House as we pulled away and sent a silent promise to return the next day. I still didn't fully understand what happened, but I knew my work here wasn't done.

18

*W*hen I cracked open my eyes, the first thing I noticed was I definitely could have used some more sleep. The second thing was that the feeling of dread that had been shadowing me for days was gone. I stretched and looked over at Zane. He was flat on his back and snoring to beat the band, so I eased out of bed and padded into the kitchen.

Bernie was already there, staring wistfully at the cupboard where I kept his food. He chirped as I walked in and rubbed his head against my leg.

"Hungry, bud? Even after all that steak?"

I'd saved him a couple of chunks of meat from our celebratory dinner the night before. What can I say? I'm a sucker. That dinner had run long into the night, but it was one of the best times I'd had in a long time.

"Those were mere morsels."

"True story. And a being of your type requires more food than that. I get you."

I dished up his food and fired up the coffee, as I pondered what we needed to do today. By the time Bernie was done with his breakfast, I was sipping on my first cup of the day.

I waited until he was done washing up before starting my question fest.

"So, we need to go back to the Maddison House today and see if we can help any of the ghosts move on. Do you want to come with me?"

"Absolutely. Don't even dream of leaving me out of it. We also need to help William and Peter."

I perked up at the names of the ghosts who'd been consumed by the wraith. Even though it was awesome that we'd bested the creature, the thought that we'd somehow lost their souls saddened me.

"You think we can help them? I thought when a wraith consumed a soul, they were gone forever."

He stopped bathing and lowered his foot to the ground before looking at me earnestly.

"Remember when I said there was justice in this world? I have to believe we can still help them. There's only one way to find out. Are you going to have Zane tag along?"

I glanced down the hall to where Zane was currently sleeping and shook my head.

"I'm not sure. I've asked an awful lot of Zane the past few days. Besides, I think he's meeting with his new client and Logan this morning. I should probably go wake him up, so he's not late."

Bernie returned to his ablutions while I snagged a cup of coffee for Zane. I carried it back to the bedroom, only spilling it once, and set it down on the table next to the bed. I sat on the bed and brushed Zane's long hair off his face gently. His nose twitched and his eyes sprang open. Once he focused on me, he gave me a smile that curled my toes.

"Good morning, beautiful," he said, leaning up to kiss me on the cheek. "Did you sleep okay?"

I nodded as I picked up his coffee cup and handed it over.

"Like a log. How about you?"

"I was down for the count. You're sure you're okay after what happened?"

He was running his hand up and down my arm as if he was searching for breaks. I smiled and patted his knee.

"Fit as a fiddle. I thought for sure I'd have nightmares, but I guess this chapter is all but complete."

"You're going to see if Arabella is ready to move on?" Zane asked before taking a sip of his coffee and closing his eyes in bliss.

"I am. I'll do that while you meet with Logan."

"After you're done, why don't you head to Creekside and meet us? I want you to go over the project and make sure it's something you want to do. By the time you're done, Logan and I should be ready."

"Sounds perfect to me. I'm going to heat those pastries, if you're hungry?"

"You know the way to my heart," Zane said as he swung his legs off the bed and stood with a stretch.

"I think that's my line," I said, giggling as I walked back to the kitchen.

By the time he was dressed for the day, I had everything ready and plated up. Bernie, predictably, pulled the starving cat act, and I gave him a tiny nibble of my danish, before polishing it up.

I gave Zane a kiss on his way out the door and wandered back to my room to get ready for the day. As I dressed, I couldn't help but think about the Ghost Twins and what their next plans were. Hopefully, they were packing up and getting out of town, and I'd never have to deal with them again. I snorted, as I realized I'd probably just jinxed myself.

Bernie was waiting for me by the door when I walked back out and grabbed my bag.

"Okay, bud, let's get this show on the road."

"I thought you'd never ask."

I sang along to the radio as we drove, feeling lighter than I had for a week. The morning sun lit up the foliage of the trees, bathing everything in a rich auburn glow. Yep, I definitely needed to take Zane on a scenic cruise before the leaves fell.

I parked in front of the Maddison House and turned off my car, while looking up at the brick facade of the building. I couldn't believe it had only been a few days since all of this began, but I was glad the worst of it was over. I grabbed Bernie's bag and headed inside, smiling at Norma as I walked in.

"Good morning. I hope you don't mind me stopping in. I see the film crew got everything cleaned up," I said.

"It's like they were never here. I still can't believe it. I almost thought I was dreaming when I walked in this morning."

She wasn't kidding. There was no trace of the multiple cameras, but I saw a few grains of salt left on the rug where we'd held the seance. I turned back to Norma, noticing she didn't appear drawn. Even if she hadn't been aware of the wraith stalking the premises, it must have impacted her. Now, there was color back in her previously faded cheeks.

"Is Russ around?"

"He's not due until later today. I think this whole thing with the board really threw him. I know it tossed me for a loop."

"I think everything will be okay. Do you mind if I go upstairs?"

"Go ahead," she said, giving me a warm smile. "I'll just be down here. We need to get everything ready for the big festival next month."

Next month would bring Halloween, and the town of Deadwood did nothing small for that holiday. There would be a fun run, music, and several days of festivities, all centered on the town's historic past. The Maddison House would be packed as people tried to get a glimpse of one of the resident ghosts. I nodded and headed up the stairs, breathing a sigh of relief at the different feel of the place.

I stopped in the hall, put Bernie's bag down, and unzipped it. He stepped out and sniffed the air, cocking his head to the side.

"They're coming," he said, sitting at my feet.

It didn't take long for the figures of four ghosts to appear, one after the other. Bessie, as usual, was first, and it warmed my heart to see her smiling. Lady Victoria wore her perpetual lemony expression, but Colonel Joseph was beaming from ear to ear as he nodded at me.

Arabella appeared last, smiling faintly, before studying the floor in front of her.

"Hello, everyone," I said, glancing over my shoulder. "Can you join me in this room?"

Even though I'm sure Norma was aware of the ghosts, I didn't want to make a scene. Bernie padded after me into the room and hopped on the bed. I looked at Bessie, but beyond puckering her lips, she didn't say a word.

"Thank you, mum," she said, avoiding looking at my cat. "Everything is ever so much better since last night. We watched from the sidelines, and we can't thank you enough."

Lady Victoria gave me a stiff nod before returning to her customary stiff position.

"Bally good job, my girl," Colonel Joseph said, his ghostly hand moving to clap me on the arm. "You were a veritable tiger."

My cheeks heated at his praise, and I shook my head.

"I don't know about that, but I'm glad I could help. I came this morning to see if anyone wanted to move on? You don't have to right away. I can come back any time, but I had a feeling I was needed today."

Arabella stepped forward, a shy smile lighting her sweet face.

"I'd like that very much," she said, glancing at Bessie. "Sorry, mum, but I feel like it's safe for me now. I've enjoyed my time here ever so much, but I think I'd like to go. It won't hurt, will it?"

She looked at me and I shook my head. Bernie walked up to her and rubbed against her ethereal leg. I didn't know if she could feel it, but the look of delight she gave him while bending down to pat his head made me think she could.

Bessie sniffed loudly and nodded, sending the lace of her mobcap trembling.

"I understand, my girl. I'll miss you, though. We all will."

The colonel cleared his throat, and for a second, I thought I spotted a gleam of tears in his eyes.

"Take care of yourself, Miss Arabella. Maybe sometime we will see you again," he said. "Not now, though. My favorite season is coming and I can't miss that. It's so much fun to see the kiddies gasp when they spot one of us."

Lady Victoria wafted closer to Arabella, sizing her up with a glance. She nodded sharply and surprised me by breaking into a smile that completely altered her appearance.

"You're a good girl, Arabella. I wish you nothing but happiness. Lord knows you deserve it. You enjoy yourself, you hear?"

I looked at Bessie with a raised eyebrow and she shook her head.

"No, thank you. Until these two go, I'll be here to care for them. I don't mind. But is there something you can do for Mr. Maddison and Peter?"

I looked at Bernie and he nodded his head to the corner of the room. There, to my surprise, were two golden orbs hovering in place. My heart skipped in wonder as they floated closer. Even though they said nothing, I felt strongly that these were the souls of William Maddison and Peter. They weren't able to manifest in their earthly forms any longer, but they were still there. I wished briefly I'd been able to meet Peter, but the feeling of joy I felt from his orb as it got closer made me feel better.

"Okay, if everyone is ready, I think it's time," I said.

Bernie moved closer to me and slowly, I saw a bright light filter through the space. Arabella's face grew almost as bright as she stared into it.

"Mama? Papa?"

The hope in her voice clogged my throat with tears as she drifted closer to the light. The orbs joined her, zipping back and forth in what I assumed was happiness. I could make out a few people standing in the distance, waiting to welcome them to their ultimate home. Arabella made eye contact one last time before walking into the light. Her expression said more than words ever could as she faded away. The light slowly dimmed before disappearing all together.

"That was beautiful," Lady Victoria said, her pointed jaw quivering ever so slightly.

"I never thought I'd see the day," the Colonel said, clearing his throat again.

"Are you sure you won't change your mind? If you're ready, I can help."

"No, but I may change my mind," Lady Victoria said, still looking up at the corner of the room. "I did not know."

One by one, the ghosts faded from view and I drew a deep breath, still overcome with emotion at what I'd seen in Arabella's eyes. It didn't matter how many times I assisted ghosts in their crossing, it still had a profound impact.

"Well, Bernie. I guess it's time to head to Creekside."

He chirped as he sped ahead of me into the hall. I got him zipped back into his carrier and headed down the stairs. I said a quick goodbye to Norma and asked her to have Russ call me. I could tell him the good news later.

The sun was shining brightly as I walked outside and I felt like I was floating on air as I walked to my car. I got in and let Bernie out before rolling down the window and pulling out of my parking space.

I turned onto the highway and cranked the music again, singing as loudly as I dared. Bernie even joined in a few times, making sure we killed every chorus. I was almost in town when my phone rang. I turned down the stereo and answered it, smiling when I saw it was from Zane.

"Hi, honey. I'm almost there."

"Good. Did everything go okay at the museum?"

"It was perfect. I can't wait to tell you. Is everything okay?"

He paused and I could almost see him trying to put his thoughts into words. He finally gave a sharp sigh.

"I wish I knew. Let's just say this is your expertise. How close are you?"

"I'll be there in five minutes."

"See you then. Logan and I are outside."

He ended the call, and I looked over at Bernie, who was listening to our conversation with perked ears.

"What do you make of that?" I asked.

"I think we're heading full speed to our next adventure," he said, curling up on the seat. "Wake me when we get there. I have a feeling I'm going to need a power nap."

I laughed to myself as I drove. I knew whatever it would be, I was surrounded by love and support, and we'd meet it head on, together.

DON'T MISS THE FRIGHT IN THE FAMILY ROOM!

Something isn't right in this Victorian house...

When Zane's new client reports strange things happening in his new house, at first they thought it was the product of paranoia. Now, the gang isn't so sure. Join Brynn and Bernie as they get ready to tackle their strangest case yet!

Get your copy now!

BOOKS BY COURTNEY MCFARLIN

Escape from Reality Cozy Mystery Series

Escape from Danger

Escape from the Past

Escape from Hiding

A Razzy Cat Cozy Mystery Series

The Body in the Park

The Trouble at City Hall

The Crime at the Lake

The Thief in the Night

The Mess at the Banquet

The Girl Who Disappeared

Tails by the Fireplace

The Love That Was Lost

The Problem at the Picnic

The Chaos at the Campground

The Crisis at the Wedding

The Murder on the Mountain

The Reunion on the Farm

The Mishap at the Meeting - Summer 2023

A Soul Seeker Cozy Mystery

The Apparition in the Attic

The Banshee in the Bathroom

The Creature in the Cabin

HAVE YOU READ THE RAZZY CAT COZY MYSTERY SERIES?

The Body in the Park
A Razzy Cat Cozy Mystery

"I'm a cat lover and read many cat mysteries. Courtney McFarlin's Razzy Cat Cozy Mystery Series is my favorite."

She's found an unlikely consultant to help solve the crime. But this speaking pet might just prove purr-fect...

Hannah Murphy yearns for a real news story. But after a strange migraine results in an unexpected ability to talk to her cat, she must keep the kitty-communication skills a secret if she wants to advance from fluff pieces to covering felonies. And when she literally trips over a slain body, she's shocked her feline companion is the best partner to crack the case.

Convinced she's finally got her big break, Hannah quickly runs afoul of a handsome detective and his poor opinion of interfering reporters. And when she discovers the victim's penchant for embezzlement and fraud, she may need more than a furry friend and a cantankerous cop to avoid ending up in the obits.

Can Hannah catch a killer before her career and her life are dead and buried?

The Body in the Park is the delightful first book in the Razzy Cat cozy mystery series. If you like clever sleuths, light banter, and talking animals, then you'll love Courtney McFarlin's hilarious whodunit.

More reader comments: "The Razzy Cat series is a joy to read! I have read the first three, and just bought the fourth. These books are well written, engaging stories. I love the positive and supportive relationships depicted amongst the main characters and the cats. That is so refreshing to read. I look forward to more books in this series. I will also be reading some this author's other works. Well done, and keep writing!" - Ingrid

Buy *The Body in the Park* for the long arm of the paw today!

Keep reading for a sneak peek at Chapter One.

BONUS: CHAPTER ONE OF THE BODY IN THE PARK

Friday, June 19th

The hum of the newsroom refused to fade into the background as I worked to file my last story for the day. I'd been assigned a fluff piece, which I usually hated, but considering it was almost the weekend, I wouldn't complain too much. I was looking forward to two blissful days off and some quality time away from work.

I've been working at the paper here in Golden Hills, Colorado, for two years, ever since I graduated from the local college. I'm originally from a tiny town in South Dakota, and I love living so close to the mountains. I'd discovered a love of hiking while I was in college, and I couldn't imagine leaving to go back home to the family farm. There's nothing wrong with farming, we all gotta eat, but for me, I needed mountains and adventure.

I read through my story one more time, checking for errors, stopping to admire my byline. Hannah Murphy, that's me. Seeing my name in print never got old. I hit enter on my laptop, posting my story to my editor with plenty of time to spare on my deadline. I rummaged around under my desk, looking for my purse. With any luck, I'd be able to slip away a bit early and head home. I poked my head over my cubicle and looked over at the glass office where my editor, Tom Anderson, was banging away on his computer. I stifled a laugh. Tom was old school, from a time when the clerical girls typed everything on typewriters, and he resented being forced to use a computer.

I grabbed my things and headed down three cubicles to where my best friend, Ashley Wilson, worked. Ashley was my roommate in college, and we were both journalism majors. While she lived for the lifestyle pages, I was drawn to the hard news and wanted to make a name for myself as a reporter. I wasn't kidding myself. I knew it was a miracle our little newspaper had its doors open still. Most small newspapers had folded years ago, and it was tough for an independent outfit to keep the lights on. But I was hoping with some luck, perseverance, and hard work, I'd be able to move up the ranks to a serious news position.

I tapped on the wall of Ashley's cubicle and flopped into the chair across from her desk.

"Hey, Ash, you about done for the day?"

Her tongue was poking out from between her lips as she focused on her screen, ignoring me. I leaned over to see what was engrossing her and saw she was working on an image in Photoshop. Since we were such a small paper, most of us had to do our design work for our stories, which wasn't always fun.

I watched her as she worked, admiring her long brown hair that was impossibly straight and glossy. My hand went up to my unruly nest of blonde locks, and I gave a rueful smile. No matter how often I tried to straighten my hair, it never turned out as pretty as hers.

We were complete opposites. She was tall, statuesque, and dark, while I was short, thin, and fair. She enjoyed shopping and partying, while I was an outdoors kind of girl. It didn't matter, though. I'd never had a friend as close as her. She gave a little shout and hit save, turning to face me.

"Hey Hannah, sorry about that. The image didn't want to cooperate."

"No worries, been there, done that. What are your plans for tonight? Are you hanging out with Bill, or was it Will?"

"Will. He was also three guys ago. You gotta keep up, girl!"

"Sorry, are you hanging out with what's his face tonight?"

"I was unless you wanted to do something. We need a girl's night out."

"We do, but not tonight. I think I've got a migraine coming on. I'll just go home and hang out with my cat."

Ashley made a sad face and heaved a sigh.

"That's how it starts. You're in your twenties, and you spend a Friday night alone, with just a cat for company. Before I know it, you'll be my crazy cat lady friend who becomes a shut-in and only leaves to buy more cat food."

"Wow, that's a depressing and strangely detailed future look."

"I call them as I see them. I kid, Hannah. You should get out more, though," Ashley said, giving me a look.

"I know, I'm just not a peopley person. I enjoy being outside, not cramped in a loud bar with sweaty people being all, I don't know, sweaty. I like my cat. I like quiet."

"I need to find you a man. I think Will had a brother..."

"Thanks, but no thanks. I don't want to get set-up with a cast-off's brother. That would be even sadder than being home alone with my cat. Seriously though, have fun tonight. I expect a play-by-play tomorrow."

Her phone rang, cutting off our conversation. I waved as I grabbed my bag to leave. It looked like the coast was clear, so I headed towards the door, determined to make a break for it. I wasn't lying to Ashley, my head was pounding, and I wanted to get home and change into my jammies.

"Hannah! Wait!"

I groaned when I heard Tom's voice, turning in my tracks to head back to his office. I stopped in the doorway.

"Hi, Tom. How was my article? Does it need any edits?"

"It was fine. You self-edit well. That's not why I wanted to talk to you," Tom said, gesturing for me to come in and take a seat.

I plopped in the comfy chair across from his desk.

"What's up?"

The way Tom dressed was as old school as the way he typed. His button-down shirt was turned up at the cuffs, exposing a myriad of ink stains. He had a nice face, utterly at odds with his gruff voice. He scrubbed his bald head and leaned back in his chair. He looked at me closely for a beat.

"Hannah, you've been doing a great job lately. I know fluff pieces aren't what you want to do, and I appreciate you've been good about working on them. I can tell you put the effort in, even though you don't enjoy the subject."

"Thanks, Tom, that's nice of you to say."

"I'd like to try you out on a few tougher pieces. The next big story that breaks is yours."

"Are you serious? I'd love to try some harder news pieces!"

This was the most exciting thing to happen to me in months. I was finally going to sink my teeth into some meaty stories!

"That and whatever else you can dig up. I know you're young, but I think you deserve a shot."

"Thank you so much. I won't let you down."

"See that you don't."

With that, he waved me off and turned back to his computer, cursing under his breath as he started banging on the keys again.

I floated out of his office, almost forgetting my headache. I got to the parking lot and climbed into my ancient Chevy Blazer. I'd saved up my money back in high school, and it was old back then. It'd seen me through college, though, and with any luck, it would get me through until I could make enough money to replace it.

Traffic was picking up as I navigated my way back to my apartment. Golden Hills was growing fast, but I was lucky enough to find a place that backed right onto a huge green space. I had acres and acres of wilderness to explore via the trail that led to the Crimson Corral park. It wasn't cheap, but it was worth it to have an outdoor space and a killer view.

I trudged up to the top floor, feeling my headache get worse with every step. By the time I made it to my door, I was feeling odd. I walked in and immediately tripped over my cat, Razzy. I'd had her for two years, ever since I got my place. I scooped her up and cuddled her close, apologizing for tripping over her. She was a Ragdoll cat, and I had no idea how a beautiful, purebred cat like her had ended up in an animal shelter.

Her soft fur felt like a rabbit, and her little purrs made me smile. She was a quiet cat who rarely meowed. I put her down and walked to the kitchen, trying to decide what to make for supper. A quick check of the fridge revealed I needed to do some serious grocery shopping. As I stood in front of my cabinets, a wave of nausea and dizziness rushed through my body. I gripped the counter to keep from falling over.

Razzy meowed at me, cocking her head to the side. It was like she could tell something was wrong. I skipped dinner and walked back to my bedroom, holding my head. I changed into my favorite pair of fuzzy pajama pants and a tank top. Maybe if I just lay down for a few minutes, I'd feel better. I collapsed onto the bed, and Razzy jumped up next to me, snuggling close. Closing my eyes, I felt darkness rush towards me.

* * *

"Mama? Mama!"

A small voice pulled me from the darkness. I blinked open my eyes, trying to get my bearings. I felt grass underneath my feet. I looked around and realized I was in a park. My stomach felt hollow as I looked around, trying to figure out why I was outside. I glanced down and saw I was still wearing my fuzzy pants and smiled. This must be a dream. At least, in my dream, I didn't have my headache.

"Mama?"

There was that voice again. I looked through the gloom, trying to see if a child was wandering around. This was a strange dream for sure.

"Mama! There you are."

A small figure walked towards me and sat in front of me, looking up into my face. It took me a second to recognize my cat, Razzy, sitting there. Her whiskers bristled in the faint light from the moon.

"Say something, Mama. You're scaring me. Why are you outside?"

I felt my world rock as I realized Razzy was talking to me. Like, really talking. I laughed when I remembered I was dreaming. Geez, this was one crazy dream. I shrugged and went with it.

"Razzy, what are you doing in my dream?"

"Um, I'm pretty sure you're not dreaming. I followed you out of the apartment. You left the door open, which isn't safe, by the way. I tracked you here and kept calling you until I found you. Why didn't you answer me?"

Ok, this was weird. She was talking to me like she was a human, and I could understand everything she was saying. This had to be the winner for my strangest dream ever.

"You were calling for mama. I figured there was a little kid in my dream who was looking for their mother. I didn't know it was you."

"I always call you that. To me, you are my mama," Razzy said, her eyes rounding with concern. "This is weird, though. I always try to talk to you, but it's like you can't understand me. Why are you suddenly understanding what I say?"

"Must be the dream. I'm sure I'm going to wake up any second and find you cuddled up next to me."

"You're not dreaming, but whatever. Can we go home now? It's getting cold."

Razzy fluffed up her fur and turned to her left, looking at me expectantly. Her tail curled into a question mark as I stood there, staring at her. Well, maybe if I followed her, I'd wake up. I must have had something bad for lunch.

I shrugged and followed her.

"Lead on, MacDuff," I said, as I fell in behind her.

"It's actually 'Lay on, MacDuff,'" Razzy said with a sniff. "Humans, always misquoting things."

"Wait, you know Shakespeare?"

"I know way more than you might think."

I couldn't help but laugh. I had a talking cat who was also a literary critic in this dream. I needed to write this down when I woke up.

Razzy paused, her tail going stiff and then curling down behind her. Her hackles went up, and she sniffed the air.

"Stop, there's something up ahead."

"Are we going to meet a talking dog next? That would be pretty cool."

I moved past her, ready to get out of this dream and wake up back in my apartment. I took a few more steps and fell over something stretched across the sidewalk. As I felt around to see what I'd tripped over, my hand came in contact with something cold and squishy. With a little shriek, I scooted back. This dream had taken a disturbing turn.

I felt in the pocket of my pajama pants and grabbed my cellphone. Switching on the flashlight app, I held it out in front of me, my hands shaking. I wasn't sure I wanted to see what it illuminated.

There, next to me on the ground, was the body of a man. I placed my fingers on his neck and felt nothing there. Jumping up, I screamed, convinced now was the perfect time for me to wake up. I looked over at Razzy. She walked closer, sat down, and shook her head.

"I told you, you're not dreaming. You should probably call the cops."

Realization flooded through me as I took stock of the situation. My feet were freezing on the cold concrete. I checked my arms and noticed I had goosebumps. I pinched myself and winced when I clearly felt it.

Razzy walked over to my feet and gently bit down on the top of my foot.

"Ouch! Why did you do that?" I asked, rubbing my foot.

"You didn't seem to believe me you're awake. You were pinching yourself, so I thought it would help if I pitched in too." She gave what I assumed to be the cat version of a shrug. "Call the cops."

I hesitated for a second before numbly obeying her suggestion and punching 9-1-1 in on my phone.

Get your copy now to read the rest!

A NOTE FROM COURTNEY

Thank you for taking the time to read this novella. If you enjoyed the book, please take a few minutes to leave a review. As an independent author, I appreciate the help!

If you'd like to be first in line to hear about new books as they are released, don't forget to sign up for my newsletter. Click here to sign up! https://bit.ly/2H8BSef

A LITTLE ABOUT ME

Courtney McFarlin currently lives in the Black Hills of South Dakota with her fiancé and their two cats.

Find out more about her books at:
www.booksbycourtney.com

Follow Courtney on Social Media:

https://twitter.com/booksbycourtney

https://www.instagram.com/courtneymcfarlin/

https://www.facebook.com/booksbycourtneym

Made in the USA
Monee, IL
27 November 2024

71453013R00097